MW00935574

WHY SHE LIED

ॐ

JULIE COONS

Copyright © 2019 by Julie Coons

All right reserved.

No part of this book may be reproduced in any form or by any electronic or mechanical means, including information storage and retrieval systems, without written permission from the author, except for the use of brief quotations in a book review.

❧ CONTENTS ❧

Chapter 1 - 1

Chapter 2 - 10

Chapter 3 - 20

Chapter 4 - 28

Chapter 5 - 38

Chapter 6 - 50

Chapter 7 - 58

Chapter 8 - 63

Chapter 9 - 83

Chapter 10 - 100

Chapter 11 - 118

Chapter 12 - 131

Chapter 13 - 143

Chapter 14 - 150

Chapter 15 - 163

Chapter 16 - 171

❧ 1 ❦

I love when the sun shines in the windows. Especially these windows. A full wall of floor-to-ceiling windows. It always gives me such a peaceful feeling to look out and see a sunny beach while sitting on the slope of a flower-filled hillside, feeling the warm breeze across my face. I frequently stare out these windows and imagine the feeling of warm sand between my toes with the sound of ocean waves crashing nearby. I look out these windows and dream I'm somewhere, anywhere else. It's a much-needed escape from an otherwise cold and sterile environment. I often propel myself into different worlds of my choosing when the world I am currently in is so filled with pain and sadness. *Anywhere but here.*

This place is such a war zone sometimes. The sounds are indescribable. They can penetrate deep inside your mind and last forever. The cry of a mother when she is told her child didn't make it. It's a shocking sound to hear, and impossible to replicate. I've never heard anything like it. I'm seeing things I was never meant to see. My mind can't take it. Luckily for me, I have a wild imagination, and daydreaming is my specialty. I work as an admitting clerk in the busiest trauma center on the West Coast.

I'm an empath, and I fear I will never get over what's happening here today. A teenage boy was in a major wreck on his motorcycle and just died. His family arrived in time to hear him pronounced dead. His brother was so distraught with grief he couldn't get out of the hospital fast enough. He ran through my work station and jumped over the counter with one long leap. The only way out of the emergency room was through a pair of automatic sliding glass doors. Unfortunately, they didn't open fast enough. He was so desperate to pry them open he pushed too hard. It sounded like an explosion when both doors shattered to the ground spreading broken glass all over the waiting room. Poor guy was just trying to escape the horror. A few moments later the Hospital Administrator came to see what happened. She was so irate when she saw all the broken glass she began yelling and threatened to sue this poor kid for breaking the glass doors. "He is going to pay for this." She repeated this over and over again as she stomped through the mess making more of a scene then the boy did. I was so angered by her lack of compassion for this family. I wanted to say something to her but I was afraid I would jeopardize my job if I didn't keep my mouth shut. However, after a few more minutes of listening to her rant I couldn't help myself. "Have a heart, he just lost his brother." She turned and glared at me for a moment then walked away without saying another word. Maybe she realized how ridiculous she looked. I couldn't believe her lack of empathy. She acted as if the money to fix the doors was coming out of her own pocket. I was just relieved her rage hadn't turned on me. At the same time, in another trauma room, a mother learned that her husband abused her baby so badly we had to life flight him to another hospital just to give him a chance to survive. The police walked her husband, now in handcuffs, right in front of me and out the door. I learned today that abused babies don't cry, they whimper.

I look around me and I see sadness and despair everywhere. I want so badly to stand up and run out those broken doors in front of me because behind me, in the war zone, things are falling apart fast. We just got another call from the ambulance service … but this time it was coming from the red trauma phone. Multiple trauma, that's what that phone is for. Code blue alarms going off throughout the hospital, calling for available staff because someone is trying to die on the fourth floor. *I can't escape.* I'm a single mother and I really need this job. I may never escape this place or the hell that awaits me, day after day. I used to think that hell was a place far beneath the earth, but sometimes I suspect it's right here. Besides needing money for bills, I'm also paying the hospital back fifteen thousand dollars from when my daughter was a patient here and nearly lost her life to spinal meningitis. I'm not even getting the child support I was ordered, and every time the court catches up to her deadbeat father's current employer, he quits and moves on to another job. I don't have a choice.

Just a few minutes ago, the baby's mother was escorted out by the police, too. He's all alone now and fighting for his little life. We just learned that both of his parents are being accused of abusing him. How unbelievable and intensely tragic but, sadly, not out of the ordinary. I had the honor of holding and comforting him before he was taken away by life flight. Later, the receiving hospital called to let us know he didn't make it. This poor child didn't even have a chance to live, and what little time he did have was spent in pain and fear.

These are the things I take home with me every night.

I've seen the worst of humanity, but I've also seen the best in people, and even some miraculous things, too. People are living some of the worst moments of their lives right in front of me. However, there are miracles in the ER, too. An elderly woman was just pronounced dead. I was doing her final preparations before she was to be taken downstairs to the morgue. I was standing next to her when all of a sudden, her head turned and, quite to my surprise, she opened her eyes and looked directly at me. I mean, she didn't just look at me, we had eye contact. I jumped back and screamed. It was such a shock to me. She'd been dead for over five minutes. A nurse in the room started to laugh and told me it's just a reflex.

This was not just a reflex.

We hadn't unhooked her from the equipment yet, and I know it's hard to believe, but her heart started beating again. Not just beating, it was beating regular and strong. Out of nowhere she sat straight up in her bed. By this time the doctor had run back into the room, looking as shocked as the rest of us. This little old lady, who'd just been dead for five minutes, started yelling and cussing out the doctor for bringing her back. I guess she liked where she was and she didn't appreciate leaving. I've never witnessed anything like it.

Every morning around three, things get really quiet in the emergency room. I used to tell my friends, if you need to go to the emergency room, try to wait and go in around three in the morning. Don't ever go to the emergency room on a Saturday night. Looking back, I was always surprised how busy things got on Sunday nights too, always around eight as well. Friday nights were surprisingly quiet. Another bad time to come into the emergency room, for reasons unknown, is during a full moon. It never failed. Horrible things happened during the full moon and we were always busy. There are things in this world I will never understand, and I witnessed quite a few of them while working in the emergency room.

If you were a sheltered child growing up, go work in the ER, it will un-shelter you real fast. I also learned that heart attacks usually come in between five and six in the morning. It's a very strange phenomena, and to the best of my knowledge, nobody has been able to explain it yet. Sometimes, late at night when things were quiet, the nurses would entrust the admitting staff to triage patients as they came in. They wouldn't be that far away, and we could always call for help, so that was reassuring. However, I never really understood nor agreed with this. It made me a little nervous.

I'm not trying to throw the fine people of the emergency room under the bus, but I think it created some kind of liability to let people without a medical license make a life or death determination. I had some nursing school experience, but I never felt comfortable triaging patients. Another thing that drove me crazy was the amount of "non-emergencies" that came into the ER. How is a sore throat an emergency? There were many instances when I felt sicker than the person I was admitting.

Later that night after most of the trauma calmed down, we were finally able to take a breath when a man came in with just that, another sore throat patient. He appeared totally normal and didn't seem to be in any distress. I sat him down at a computer so I could get him registered. All of a sudden, his expression changed and he began to look at me in a very angry sort of way. I asked him if everything was all right. I sat for an uncomfortable amount of time waiting for him to answer me when he turned and looked at absolutely nothing next to him and said, "You be quiet, I'm doing the talking."

Like I said, working here was rarely boring. I excused myself and quickly ran to get some help. I'm not sure what his diagnosis was, but I certainly got a scary vibe from him. About a half hour after he was taken back to the treatment area, a huge group of police officers showed up. That was nothing new, we always had police coming in and out of the ER. We had a large cafeteria downstairs, and they liked to come eat here because the food was good and very cheap. They usually came in through the back door where the ambulances brought in the patients. Tonight, however, they came running in through the front door. I could hear officers yelling out commands, so I just had to go see what was going on. The police had surrounded the strange man and had him in handcuffs. Finally, after everything settled down, I was told he was wanted for murder. Not just one but several murders. Our evening nurse recognized him from a story she saw on the local news and called the police. Her husband was actually on the SWAT team. I was pretty freaked out because I had just been in the front triage area completely alone with this person.

Alone, with a serial killer, what a cool way to end a shift…

It's shocking to discover all the scary things that happened in my small town. Another fact I was surprised to learn from working in the emergency room … most of the drama rarely made it into the local news. One day, I had the opportunity to ask one of our administrators why. I was told if they reported everything that went on, it would cause panic within the community. I don't know if I believe that, I think the public gets a bad rap. I think people can handle more than they are given credit for. I'm sure it's true, not just for my town, but for every town in the USA. Many things that happen just aren't reported to the general public. I know for a fact that it happened where I live, so why not other places, too? Who knows, after some of the things I've seen, perhaps it would cause panic. Sometimes I wonder how close to danger I might have been in the past without even knowing it. I don't mean to sound paranoid, but I've seen some things.

Unfortunately, my little town experienced a few horrible events that made it all the way up to national news.

Back in the 60's, there was a serial killer named Jerome Brudos. He was a murderer and necrophile who killed several women in Oregon. He was best known as "The Shoe Fetish Killer," or "The Lust Killer." Brudos lived in my town, on Center St., not too far from the hospital where I worked. To say he was a deeply disturbed individual would be an understatement. I read a book written by Ann Rule about him after he was caught. One day, I was driving by his old home on Center Street when I noticed that not only was it on the market, the realtor was there holding an open house. It took some courage, but I managed to park my car and go inside. I could picture it exactly as it was described in Ann's book. The rafters in the garage where he hung the girls, the ledge next to the fireplace where he displayed the "paperweights" he made with his victims' own breasts. The freezer in the garage where he kept the body parts. It was incredibly creepy just standing inside this garage because I knew what kind of horror took place there. I used to attend the same church as one of his victims. Her name was Karen. Her father went to my dad's men's clothing store to buy a new suit to wear to her funeral. Karen's father told mine that his family wouldn't be coming back to our church. I strongly resembled Karen, and it was just too painful for her family to have to look at me every Sunday.

On another night, I was on my way home after getting off work around ten. I was driving down the main road through Keizer, Oregon. Keizer is a newly incorporated small bedroom town just outside of Salem. I noticed up ahead, near another intersection, more police officers than I'd ever seen before. Being more interested in getting home, I continued on my way instead of trying to investigate. I enjoy taking the back roads home through different neighborhoods instead of staying on the main drag. So, instead of driving a little further up the main road to see what was going on, I took the first left. As I made my way through the neighborhood I came upon an S-curve in the road. At this point, I was about a half mile away from the intersection with all the police activity. When I got to the middle of the S-curve my headlights locked on a man walking down the sidewalk. He was wearing

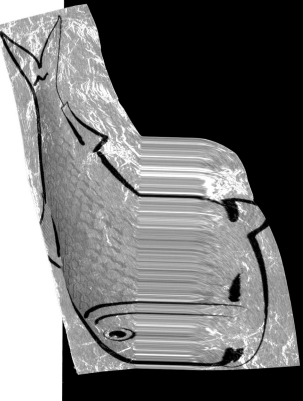

a hooded jacket. I looked at him and he stared right back at me. It was a little creepy the way he looked at me. It was more than just a glance. I tried not to think too much of it and went home. However, the way our eyes met, and the look in his ... it really startled me and I can honestly say it haunted me for a period of time. The next night while watching the evening news, I saw a composite drawing of the same individual I'd seen the night before. The news reporter said he was wanted for questioning in relation to a recent murder.

I was only seventeen at the time, so I told my parents I'm sure I saw this man on my way home from work last night. My parents encouraged me to report it to the police. The officer I spoke with asked me if I thought I would be able to pick him out of a lineup. I said, "Yes, absolutely." I never heard from the police again. A few months later I found out the person in question was Randall Woodfield, aka "The I-5 Bandit." This individual was wanted for questioning in several murders. After he was apprehended, he admitted to the police that he'd been on a murderous killing spree through California, Oregon, and Washington, which claimed forty-four lives. The worst part of my experience was when I found out that the girl he murdered *the same night I saw him* was also a friend of mine from high school.

I saw him on the road that night so clearly that every time they showed him on the news, I still recognize those eyes. I often wondered why he was walking down the street that night. Was he coming back to the scene of his gruesome crime? Where was he coming from? Could he have been in my neighborhood stalking his next victim? It seemed weird because the way we looked at each other was more intense than anything I remember experiencing before. This seemed endless ... longer than what is natural, and creepy because at that very moment, I felt something quite chilling go through my body. It was a bizarre feeling of something ominous just from looking into someone else's eyes, that I couldn't quite understand. I couldn't wrap my head around what it was because I didn't know at the time ...

I was looking into the soul of a killer.

My classmate Shari from high school was murdered by Woodfield. She was cleaning an insurance office located on the main street in Keizer. Her father owned a janitorial company and Shari and her

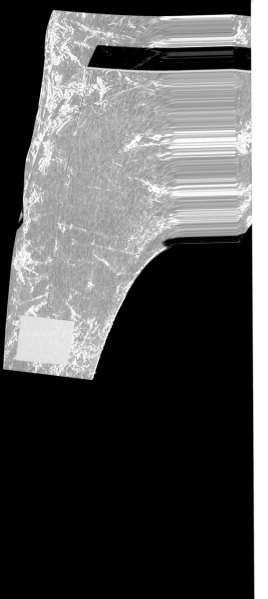

friend Lisa worked for him. Shari was preparing to leave when she was grabbed by Woodfield who'd somehow managed to enter the building. He held them at gunpoint and led them into a back room. After sexually assaulting them, he shot them in the back of the head. Lisa survived because she had the presence of mind to play dead. I can't imagine the amount of pure bravery that took. I think Woodfield had killed before I saw him on the sidewalk that night. That's why all the police activity was happening on the main drag. I believe he was on his way back to the scene of his crime so he could observe everything that was going on. Sort of like how an arsonist stays at the scene to watch the fire. After the crime scene investigators left and the building was cleared, my father got a crew of men volunteers together to go clean the insurance company. My father did this as a favor so her father wouldn't have to see it. I was very proud of him and the other men that helped. There were so many good people in our little town. To take the time to help clean up something so horrific spoke volumes about these men.

I'm not saying it was Jerome Brudos or Randall Woodfield who came into the ER that night, but I will say it was someone equally as disturbing. When you come face to face with pure evil, it really does something to you. Everyone has their "thing" that bugs them in the ER and mine is fingers. I can't handle finger injuries or fingers that have been cut off. One night a guy came into the ER with three fingers sitting on ice inside a metal bowl. I'll never get that visual out of my head. It was like something out of a horror movie. I was expecting the fingers to start moving slowly across the ice. I could really gross you out with finger stories, but frankly, I don't want to relive it anymore.

I don't remember why I used to want to be a doctor. I can't even handle the sight of blood. One day I walked into a treatment room, just in time to see blood spurting out of a patient's arm. I ran out and headed straight for the break room in case I needed to pass out on the couch. I worked with this really cool biker chick nurse named Pam who just happened to be in the room when I freaked out. She never let me forget about it and teased me every chance she got. She said, "And you want to be a doctor?"

Oh, ok, maybe not. I never forgot the patients that were either traumas or made an impact on me. I know what a person looks like when they swan dive off the top of a six-story building and land on their face. *I will spare you the details.* I've seen way too many abused babies, mostly at the hands of their own parents. I have seen too many different ways people have tried to take their own lives. I've experienced things here that will stay with me forever. Not only have I observed the worst moments in other people's lives, this place was instrumental in laying the groundwork for when my own life took a drastic turn.

❧ 2 ❦

We had our regulars, including this one patient who came into the emergency room quite often. A sweet older woman, who suffered terribly from Lupus. Her son always came with her. One day out of the blue he asked me out on a date. It felt rather awkward and my first instinct was to say no. He asked me why, and I said something totally cheesy and unbelievable like, "We aren't allowed to date patients."

He immediately responded with, "I'm not a patient."

He kept asking me out, so I had to come up with another excuse. I told him I was still getting over a bad breakup, which wasn't a complete lie. I would have totally been on the rebound, and I was still secretly hoping TJ and I would eventually get back together again. It wouldn't be fair for me to date anyone at this point in time, so I kept turning him down. It started to actually annoy me how many times he asked me out. Can't this guy take a hint? *I don't want to go out with you.* However, why I didn't want to date him was another question. He wasn't a bad looking guy, actually he was tall, dark, and a little bit handsome. He was very nice to me and he got along really well with everyone else. All the nurses absolutely adored him. I mean, any number of them would have gone out with him and most of them told me I was crazy not to.

I used to think he almost got along too well with everyone. It made me a little leery. Even though I turned him down almost daily, we still continued to talk to each other when he came in with his mother. We talked about our families, and I told him I was divorced. One night, out of the blue, he said, "I hear you have a daughter. She's four, right?" He seemed very interested in my daughter, which surprised me a little.

My favorite subject was my daughter, so we talked a lot about kids. He seemed to really like kids, too. Not many guys will stand there and talk about children with you. They would rather talk cars or almost anything else. This guy was starting to make me think he was different and perhaps just a really good person. Maybe I was being too judgmental. Maybe I wasn't being fair to him. The fact that everyone loved him so much only made me question myself all the more.

However, there was still that nagging intuition that kept telling me not to go out with him. I've always called my intuition my "gut," and over the years I have learned the hard way to always listen to it. The times when I ignored my gut were times when I always ended up regretting it. Was it really my gut telling me not to go out with him, though? Or possibly just my own desire that someday my ex-boyfriend TJ would ride in on his white horse and rescue me away from this place. Unfortunately, life isn't a fairy tale. No white horse was coming. I didn't know it yet, but TJ was already living with his latest girlfriend and had a baby on the way.

One of the nurses came up to me one day and said, *in her lovely Irish accent ...*

"Why are you giving this poor boy such a hard time?"

I told her I really didn't want to date anyone now. I was still getting over TJ. She said, "Crap on TJ, he cheated on you and broke your heart. Here is a nice guy who desperately wants to take you out on a date. Give the boy a chance."

I even told her my gut feeling about him wasn't good and I didn't want to go out with him. Besides, I know nothing about him.

"Hogwash, you are just carrying a torch for old TJ. He's moved on and forgotten all about you."

Definitely hard to hear, but she was right. TJ had cheated on me for eight months during our relationship. I need more time, maybe I will consider dating again in about a year or so. It's just me and my daughter now. Something was still screaming at me to stay clear of this man. Was it my gut? Or was I just being paranoid?

I didn't quite understand why I kept getting such a weird vibe about going out with this person. I know by now to always listen to my intuition. However, I question everything about my decisions. I've always struggled with self-confidence and self-esteem and I was desperately lacking both since my breakup with TJ. We'd been broken up for almost a year, but my friends were right, I was still carrying a torch and hoping he would want me back someday.

Maybe it was time to move on, but was this the guy to move on with? I struggled with the nagging feeling that he certainly was not. I also worried that I was vulnerable still and an easy target to get my heart broken once again. I can't handle another bad breakup. According to everyone I worked with, however, I was wrong not to go out with him. They all thought I was making a huge mistake and passing up the opportunity of a lifetime. They treated him like he was some kind of a prince. They acted like he was "Mr. Right," but was he really "my" Mr. Right? Or perhaps he's my "Mr. Not Right Now." Personally, I think he has everyone fooled. I know this for sure, everyone thinks I'm the fool.

What should I do?

What I wasn't aware of at the time was the amount of effort he put into getting me to go out with him. I started to think the more I turned him down, the more I became a challenge and a conquest for him. Later on, I would come to learn it had very little to do with me. When he came into the ER with his mother, and I wasn't there, he worked my coworkers to talk me into going out with him. Now he's developing his own little posse.

It really got weird. I have never had so many people try to talk me into dating someone in my entire life, especially someone I wasn't even that interested in. How he managed to get all my coworkers on his side is still a mystery to me. He must have been a real charmer when I wasn't around. *Beware of the charmers.* They are just wolves in sheep's clothing most of the time. Sociopaths and psychopaths have all been described by professionals as being charmers. With all this going on, who could stand up against the scrutiny? I finally caved one night and accepted a date from him, against my better judgment. *And completely against my intuition.*

An hour before the date, I picked up the phone to cancel. My intuition, *my gut* was screaming at me not to go. *I'm losing my mind.* This is just ridiculous, I need to force myself to go out, have a good time, and put the past in the past. And that's exactly what I did. *Or, I should say, what I tried to do.* We went out on what began as a normal date, first dinner then a movie. The movie was cut short because he needed to go take care of his mother.

I wondered if she'd sabotaged his date, but I really didn't know her well enough to make that determination. Maybe she had a gut feeling, too. Maybe she was trying to save me. The only thing that bothered me was his incessant desire to talk about my daughter. I tried to slough it off, he's just trying to be nice and get on my good side. I'm being too paranoid, I just need to try to relax, let my guard down a little bit and have some fun for a change. Before he dropped me off, he asked to set up a rain check for another date. I accepted.

I started to actually like him, and I finally convinced myself I had no reason to be so critical of him. This is all about me and my own insecurities. I put my concerns away and we continued to see each other. Most of the time, he took me along with him when he had a remodeling gig. He fancied himself a jack of all trades ... a carpenter, a handy man, just about any kind of remodeling you needed, he could do it. I went along to help. Each time we went to someone's home, the homeowners were always there expressing their extreme admiration of him. He also had a daytime job at a daycare center, *I just didn't know it yet. He never shared that information with me.* I haven't given "him" a name yet. I will call him James. This isn't his real name because I am still afraid of this person. I have to protect myself.

I continued to find it really odd how many people went out of their way to praise him. If I could have gotten through an entire day without someone singing his praises, then maybe I could have put it behind me, too. Why do they feel the need to go overboard selling me on him, telling me over and over again what a great guy he is? Now I wonder if there was some payment involved, it was just that freaky weird. Again, maybe it's just me. This had never happened with anyone else I've dated before and it was starting to annoy me again. Maybe he only took me places where the people were more than happy to vouch for him. *This really should've been another red flag.* He had these close friends that lived in Washington State. Out of the blue one day, I got a call from them to congratulate me on dating James. They told me they were huge fans of his and big supporters. *Big supporters?* Why did he need support?

At the end of the conversation they added, "You better not break his heart."

Again, weird, right? What is this guy, a celebrity? What am I missing? Why am I starting to feel so uncomfortable again about dating him.

We never had many fancy dates. Mostly we just hung out at his jobs, which sounds odd, but he never spent much money on me. That was never a requirement for me, but it sounds weird that he rarely took me anywhere. We didn't spend much time at his house, either. He lived with his mother, which I also found a little strange because he was thirty-two years old. When I asked him why, he said it was because he was her caregiver. However, he didn't spend much time there. He carried a pager for her to call him if there was ever an emergency. There were no cell phones yet. I went over to their house once, and all James and his mom, Evelyn, did was fight, so I didn't stick around long. He never said much about their relationship, but I could tell he hated her. They lived in our little town's version of the "other side of the tracks." People referred to this neighborhood as "felony flats." It was low-income housing and close to the prison. Many former prisoners of the Oregon State penitentiary lived there when they got out of prison.

The area never gave me a sense of security, so I didn't spend much time there. I never would've brought my daughter there, that's for sure. He started getting upset that I rarely allowed him around her. The entire time we dated, he was only around Stephanie once. We met him at a pancake house for breakfast. He insisted on sitting next to her, bought her some hot chocolate and, in my opinion, went way overboard trying to get her to like him. *It made me very uncomfortable.* She was only four, and she liked that he bought her hot chocolate, but nothing much other than that.

I felt uncomfortable having her around him, so that was the only time she was. *Why was I feeling so uneasy when he was with my daughter?* It was really mother's intuition, but at the time I just chalked it up to me being an overly protective mother, and I didn't want her involved until I knew we were serious. I'd observed too many of my friends bring their children into their relationships much too soon, and when they broke up, the children felt abandoned. I have even seen some kids blame themselves for the breakup. I didn't want that for Stephanie, so I made sure to protect her from it.

What I don't understand is, why wasn't I also worrying about protecting myself? Why did I keep ignoring my own intuition? Mine is a cautionary tale. The moral to my story is … always listen to your gut. My intuition was trying to save me.

If only I had listened.

***

One evening we were hanging out at my apartment eating popcorn and watching old movies. I only allowed him to come over when Stephanie was away for her weekend visits with her father. This wasn't unusual, I did it this way with my ex-boyfriend TJ, too. TJ and I met at the hospital a couple years after my divorce from Stephanie's father. TJ was a police officer and made frequent trips to the ER. The entire two years we were together, TJ was only around Stephanie once, too. By this time, James and I had only been dating for about three months. "Julie, it's getting really late, can I crash here tonight?"

"Ok, but you will have to sleep on the couch." I wasn't inviting any man into my bed who I'd only dated for a little over three months. This probably sounds terribly old fashioned and outdated, but I told everyone I was waiting for marriage because my religion was against pre-marital sex. But the truth is, I'm broken. I don't like sex. I'd been brutally raped in the past and it just wasn't my thing. I don't have a sex drive. How could anyone ever enjoy doing that? I can't even begin to understand it when people say they love sex.

Am I a huge anomaly in this world, or could there be others out there like me? My first sexual experience was a violent rape. Who would have a sex drive after that? If my friends weren't already worried enough about me, this new revelation caused them to wonder what's wrong with me even more. All I can say is, walk a mile in my shoes before you judge me. Chances are, I probably need way more counseling than money can buy. Is there even a name for this? I'm the polar opposite of a sex addict.

Ask me how many boyfriends I've lost already...

***

I woke up in the middle of the night with a jolt because James was lying next to me in bed. He was trying to snuggle up to me and I knew what he was trying to do.

"No James, I don't want to have sex, I'm not on any kind of protection right now." I kept telling him no but he wouldn't stop.

"Don't worry Julie, "I'll be careful, I won't get you pregnant."

Oh sure, famous last words.

I tried to push him off of me but he was too strong. I started to yell at him and eventually I started hitting him on his back. Nothing deterred him, he just became more determined and a whole lot stronger. The whole time he was trying to calm me down and kept telling me *over and over again* not to worry, he'd be careful and not get me pregnant. I kept trying to push him off of me or wiggle out from under him, but I just couldn't. I felt so trapped but mostly, I felt really angry. By the time I pushed him off of me it was too late. I didn't know it yet, but I would soon learn my worst fears had come true. He had indeed gotten me pregnant.

This isn't a compliment to him at all, but it was the fastest sex I have ever had. Plus, can I even call it rape? Now I think I was raped, but I didn't want to call it rape. I didn't know what to call it. I was raped in college and I absolutely knew then, it was rape. He was a stranger, waited for a victim inside my locked dorm, held a butcher knife to my throat, and raped me. He told me after he raped me he was going to kill me.

There was no question about that, however, this was different. I knew him, we were dating, and I had allowed him to spend the night in my apartment. Is there a word for this? I kicked him out of my apartment and told him I never wanted to see him again. In the end, I never called it rape. I just did what came natural for me and blamed myself for letting him stay the night. Years later I heard a term called, "date rape." That's exactly what this is called.

But this wasn't even close to the worst thing that happened to me since meeting James, not by a long shot.

***

About two days later he came to see me, begging for forgiveness, and told me it would never happen again. *I should've known better.* How many times did I hear those same exact words from my ex-husband? Every time I left him after he got drunk and beat the crap out of me … every single time, I heard those words from him. It will never happen again. *Famous last words.* The same words spoken now by two different people. My problem is, I'm too forgiving. I have a long history of forgiving people, starting at a very early age with my own abusive mother. I was raised by an abusive, narcissistic and mentally ill mother. She frequently told me "Your father never wanted you" and "I wish you had died at birth." She used to whisper in my ear how I would find her dead when I got home from school that day. She was a master at mental torture. I am more familiar with abuse than I am with anything else, so of course … I forgave him.

I told him I would give him another chance, but if anything like that ever happened again, we were through. Today I believe, after much reflection and soul searching, we teach people how we deserve or want to be treated. It's a weird concept to wrap your head around, but we really do teach people how to treat us. If you want respect from others, it has to start with yourself. Not only do you have to love yourself to love someone else, if you don't respect yourself, how can you expect others to?

I wonder what kind of message I was giving him and any other man who abused me. There goes my weak self-esteem again. I really wished I had loved myself more, and listened to my gut more, *especially my gut*, above everyone else. Things have never gone bad for me when I listened to my intuition. Every single time when I ignored it, bad things happened. I believe now that our intuition is there to protect us.

Here's a time in my life when I did choose to listen to my intuition, and it probably saved me. I wasn't even completely aware it was my intuition that saved me at the time. I was invited to an event at our local bar, The Oregon Museum. It was a major event in our town, and everyone I knew was going to be there. Something felt a little weird about it to me and I decided not to go. I can't really explain why, either. This wasn't in character for me at all. I never passed up an opportunity to socialize with my friends. It was ladies' night and a very popular band was going to be performing, too. This is definitely something I wouldn't normally miss. So many people showed up. The Oregon Museum wasn't that big of a bar, it was kind of a run-down roadhouse type of bar. It was just too small to accommodate everyone. Many people were turned away at the door. I'm sure there were some very angry people who didn't get in, too. Today they are probably considering themselves blessed. Kind of like those people who are too late to catch their plane … then later they find out that the same plane crashed to the ground. I'm sure they are counting their lucky stars. I have a bit of an idea now how that feels. I believe I was saved that night.

As the evening progressed and many people were preoccupied dancing on the dance floor, an unemployed mill worker walked into the crowded tavern, and without saying a word, started firing his 9mm semi-automatic Browning handgun. The man fired his first shot toward the bar, then turned his weapon toward the crowd, scattering the frightened customers. Once the magazine ran out, he reloaded and continued firing. While he was reloading, *thankfully for the final time*, several people at the tavern overpowered him, wrestled him to the ground, and held him down while waiting for the police to arrive. When the killing spree ended, five people were dead and twenty others were wounded.

The bar was described by witnesses as, "A scene of sprawled victims, many with massive head, chest, and leg injuries. Bloody clothing, upturned furniture, and broken glass greeted police officers. An immediate call went out to all available ambulances. Teams of medics alternated soothing words to dazed victims and frantic cries for stretchers and first aid equipment." It was the second mass shooting in Oregon. The shooter, Lawrence Moore, was convicted of aggravated murder months later. He was sentenced to four consecutive life sentences. He gave no motive for the shooting.

I remember the moment when I first learned of the shooting. I was getting into bed for the night. I usually turned on the radio for something to help me relax and listen to as I fell asleep. The first thing I heard was "breaking news" about the shooting. I was awake and worried all night, wondering about my friends who were there. I just sat up all night listening to the local radio stations reporting on the shooting. Five of my friends had been hit, and one of my friends died at the scene. I knew the owner of the bar very well because he was a customer of mine at the bank I used to work at. This event rocked our little city off its feet for a very long time. Today, the building has been torn down and the land where the tavern once stood is an empty lot, completely surrounded by a chain-link fence. I drive by there often and say a prayer for all the souls lost that fateful night. The fence is a nice touch, I think. It feels as if it's an unspoken memorial. I hope nothing ever gets built here. It should be hallowed ground. What happened here was a nightmare for many, and very well could've been where my own life ended.

Always, listen to your gut.

❧ **3** ❧

After a couple weeks and some lengthy and rather uncomfortable conversations about boundaries, James and I were getting back on track. I was helping him organize his storage unit one afternoon when a stranger walked in. *It startled me.* I was sitting in the balcony, folding blankets, and this man walked in and started talking to James. I sat there quietly, sort of hiding. I didn't know who he was, James hadn't told me he was expecting anyone, so it could be anybody. It could even be someone who was angry at James. He certainly didn't look very friendly. I couldn't really hear what they were talking about, but I could see James was acting extremely uncomfortable around this man.

The man eventually left, so I came down the stairs to ask James who he was. "Hey James, who was that?"

"He's just the manager of the storage units. He was collecting rent because I was a few days late."

However, I never once saw James give this man any money. I said to James, "You better not be lying to me."

Deep down I knew James was lying. The way this man and James appeared to be talking, it was way more important than just a little issue of a late rental fee. A few moments later James asked me to leave because he needed to get to another job. I left with a whole lot of questions, but I wasn't feeling very good, so I wanted to go home anyway.

I fear James has secrets I know nothing about…

***

I felt like I'd had the flu for about a week. It finally dawned on me: *Could I be pregnant?* Oh Lord, please, no. I can't be pregnant. Well yes, I can be pregnant, actually. What a scary thought. I went to the drugstore and bought a pregnancy test. After taking the test I just sat there and stared at it for the longest time, when it finally came up positive. I did the same thing when I found out I was pregnant with Stephanie. It's always such a shock when you find out. I was happy, though. I loved kids. I had no idea how I would afford another child, and I certainly don't know the father very well, but it's an innocent baby and, most importantly, it's my baby.

The excitement started to build. I was born to be a mother. *But now?* I had hoped I would have been married first, but that's not a requirement. Not anymore. How do I tell my parents? They couldn't handle it when I was pregnant with Stephanie, this news might actually kill them this time. I wasn't really smiling at that thought. *Maybe a little.* Although … hey, what do you expect from me? They tried to trick me into having an abortion when I told them I was pregnant with Stephanie, and when that didn't work, they tried to move me into a convent so the nuns could adopt out my baby. I don't trust them, and I'm still very much afraid of them. What new hell would this news bring my way?

I had no idea where the hell was coming from, but it was coming fast and coming from a direction I never could have anticipated.

Well now, here's an interesting twist to my story. I don't think "interesting" is the right way to describe it, how about "horrifying?" Nobody can make this stuff up, that's for damn sure. The first person I needed to tell that I was pregnant was the father. I called James and told him I had something I needed to talk to him about.

He said, "Good, because I have something I need to talk to you about, too."

We decided to meet at his house. He asked me if we could sit in his pickup truck to talk because his mother was asleep inside. I said sure, so we both got in his truck. We sat there for what felt like forever doing the "who goes first" thing. Then he started to talk. He said, "Julie, I have something very important to share with you."

I have something very important to share with you, too.

"I have been accused of something, and even though I'm completely innocent, my trial is tomorrow, and I wanted to tell you about it first."

My mind was racing. "Your trial?"

"Yes, I have a court date tomorrow, and instead of letting you read about it in the newspaper, I wanted to tell you myself."

"Ok, tell me … what's going on?"

"I was accused of molesting a child."

WHAT!!!

"OMG, you were what? *Where, when, how?* Tell me again, did I hear that right? Who accused you, who was the child, where did it happen, and why in the hell are you just now telling me about this?"

He actually said it as calmly as if he were ordering lunch, with as much emotion, and didn't seem to be the least bit affected by the enormity and the disgust of it all. He seemed so matter-of-fact, like it was just another day for him. Where was the remorse? I don't know, but I thought maybe I should just try to calm myself down a little and hear him out. My heart was racing so fast, and I felt like I was about to throw up. However, I was telling myself to calm down and hear him out, this could be an angry ex-girlfriend or someone out to hurt him. I just didn't want to come to any conclusions too quickly. *I can't believe this is happening. I came over to share that I'm pregnant, and you are telling me you're accused of doing the one most heinous, unforgivable thing on the planet.* How in the world do I tell him I'm pregnant now, and most importantly, should I even tell him?

"I worked at a day care center, and that's where it happened."

Where it happened? Did he just confess?

"What do you mean, James, *where what* happened?"

"Where I was accused of molesting a girl."

"Ok, give me a second to breathe, and then start at the beginning."

"Maybe we should take a break from all this, and you can share what you wanted to talk to me about."

I yelled over at him, "I'm pregnant!" *How did that just come flying out of me?*

"That's awesome!"

Are you freaking kidding me? I can't think of a worse time to find out I'm pregnant.

"Oh, and your court hearing is tomorrow?" *I kept questioning him, ignoring his weird excitement about my pregnancy.*

James said, "Yes."

"Can I go?"

James reluctantly said yes, but then he added, "You sure you want to?"

I told him I wanted to be there, I needed to be there. I tried to make him think it was to support him, but the truth was, I had to be there for my own sake. I still needed answers to the big question … guilty or innocent?

Then I asked him to explain to me exactly what happened. What came next is a bit of a blur. I think when times are so stressful our brains take over to protect us from what's about to come. He told me the mother had some kind of personal vendetta against him because he wouldn't go out with her. My first thought was, *who does that?* Who accuses someone of something so hideous just because they didn't want to date you? It didn't sound reasonable to me at all. I know it would never occur to me to do something like that to another person. There is nothing worse you can accuse someone of. I kept asking him to tell me about the child he was accused of molesting. I asked him to describe her, and tell me how old she was. He glossed over this information, so I kept pressing him for the truth. He said many words but I really wasn't connecting well with what he was saying until I heard him say, "A four-year-old girl."

I looked down because I had kicked a file binder on the floor of his truck. I asked him what it was. He stated those were the papers for his case. *I desperately need to get my hands on those documents.*

I asked him if he would let me take them home to read them and he said, "No."

"Why not?"

"I'm afraid you will get upset from what's in there, and it might hurt your pregnancy."

"Please, please, please James, I really want to read those documents."

"No, Julie, I won't allow it." *Won't allow it? Yeah, we'll just see about that.* Bullshit, I really need to get my hands on those papers.

In those documents lie the truth.

I told James I needed to go be alone for a while to process all of this. But in all honesty, I was absolutely driven to get my hands on those documents. *Where do I go now?* Who will help me? His attorney, maybe? No, his attorney is paid to be on his side. The District Attorney, perhaps. I drove downtown to our local courthouse. After talking with the clerk, I found out who the district attorney for his case was. The District Attorney told me I would really need to get this information from his attorney, then he asked, "What's a nice girl like you doing with a guy like this?"

I drove directly to his attorney's office and told him my dilemma. The attorney told me if James signed a release form, he would give me access to all his documents. *Bingo!* I drove right back to James' house without even bothering to call and ask if it was all right to come over. I was a woman on a mission. I was desperate to get my hands on those papers. I gathered some other papers together that I still had in my car.

My car was always a mess. I never threw anything out. I had a bad habit of throwing everything in the back seat of my car. Luckily, I had some discharge papers from a recent doctor visit still sitting on the back seat. I gathered the medical papers together, carefully stuffed the release form his attorney gave me inside, and took it over to James to sign. I told him I had just been to the doctor, my first baby check-up, and I needed him to sign a paper so the doctor would be able to give him confidential information about the pregnancy. I told him it was confidentiality authorization stuff, and that he wouldn't be allowed to access any information from my doctor unless he signed the release form.

I also told him by signing the form it made him my emergency contact person, too. He liked the sound of that. *Sucker.* I had to throw that in because I was afraid he was getting a little suspicious. Luckily, he was never the wiser. He signed the release form without even questioning it. *That was easy.* I quickly got the hell out of there and back to my mission.

A woman on a mission can accomplish anything...

Time to go back to the attorney's office and get the important information I needed. I handed him the release form and sat in the waiting room while I nervously waited for the receptionist to photocopy it for me. When she was done she handed me a huge stack of papers.

Now I had to come up with enough courage to actually read the documents. I desperately needed to know the truth so I went straight home and began to read. Each document led me down a path of horror. It really was unbelievable and beyond sickening to read. I had to take many breaks in between reading it all. It was just too much for my brain to comprehend. Was this really the person I had dated for the past three months? It read like a horror movie, and he was the monster starring in it. Between being newly pregnant and reading this, I was intensely stressed out and incredibly nauseated. I couldn't tell if it was what I was reading making me sick or the pregnancy. Honestly, I believe it was what I was reading. I grew more and more disgusted and physically ill at the turn of each page.

The first document I read told me what he was accused of, with frightening details of the accusation. "Kidnapping in the first degree and sexual assault in the first degree." My intuition was screaming, *Told you so.* He groomed this poor, innocent child in much the same manner as he did me. When I got to the description of the little girl, that's when my world really fell apart. She had the same physical characteristics as my own daughter. Long dark hair, olive colored skin, brown eyes, and to top it all off, they were exactly the same age. Each page I read made me want to kill him. I mean, literally kill him. Then I came upon the most important document. This one piece of paper held the name and phone number of the mother of his victim. *Should I reach out to her?* I don't know right now if that's a good idea or not, but I will keep this one in my hip pocket.

Then I came to the documents regarding the polygraph examination. There were three exams total, and he *miserably* failed them all. After I finished reading, there was no question, he did it. No question in my mind, he was guilty as sin. I also read some psychological evaluations that not only made me even more disgusted, *if that were even possible,* but it put a whole lot of fear into me as well. Not only did he molest a four-year-old child, the psychologist who evaluated him was concerned he had the mental capacity to be a killer.

He was diagnosed as a psychopath, sociopath, and probably many other "paths" I have forgotten. He was someone to be feared. The psychology examination told me he was a monster. He was also considered at the highest risk for reoffending. I read so many disturbing things in these papers. No wonder he "wouldn't allow it" when I asked his permission to read them. Even though I read some horrific things in these documents, the scariest part for me was the realization that his victim resembled my daughter so much. Thank God she wasn't around him more than that one time when we met for breakfast, and never once was she ever alone with him. She sure would have been alone with him if he'd had anything to say about it.

What kind of psycho was I dating?

His trial is tomorrow, first thing in the morning, eight a.m. sharp. I found someone to stay with my daughter and I headed toward the courthouse. I didn't want him to even see me walk in. I wanted to be invisible in that room. What I didn't account for was how hard it is to find parking around the courthouse, especially first thing in the morning. I finally found a parking space, but it made me a bit late, which ended up being in my best interest.

I completely froze when I got to the courtroom door. The severity of the situation became crystal clear to me as soon as I looked inside. The room was huge and felt so formal and cold. The weird smell of old wood inside the big, cold building was permeating my senses as I stood there, dazed and frozen. What was about to happen is going to completely turn my life upside down. I couldn't just stand there, though, someone would call attention to me and I didn't want to be noticed. I bravely walked inside and quietly sat down in the back row.

Ahead of me I saw James standing up, facing the judge with his attorney standing next to him. I arrived just in time to hear James say the word, "Guilty." I couldn't hear very well, but I heard that word loud and clear. I sat there stunned. He never told me he was going to admit to doing it. *Why didn't he prepare me for this?* I looked across the room, fighting the tears welling up in my eyes, when I saw a woman sitting alone across the aisle, just a few seats ahead of me. I thought to myself, that must be the mother of the victim. She was a very beautiful woman with long dark hair, small build, sitting alone looking so sad, but also with an intense look of wanting to kill the person standing in front of her.

Who could blame her? Certainly not me, I would want to kill him, too. I so desperately wanted to reach out to her, without clearly knowing why. Maybe deep down inside, *subconsciously*, I needed to talk to her. However, what I really needed right now was to get out of there before I threw up. I wasn't even there more than five minutes, but I'd heard what I needed to hear, *guilty*. I quietly snuck out of the courtroom and walked out of that dreary place, crying all the way to my car. I felt like I had just left my life shattered all over the courtroom floor.

Now what am I going to do?

⨯ **4** ⨯

A few days later, when I was able to pull myself together again, I went back to the courthouse to find out exactly what he had been convicted of. I was shocked yet again when I read the most recent legal documents. I didn't realize at the time when I was sitting there during his trial it was actually a Grand Jury trial. I'm not sure why that made it more serious to me, maybe just the "Grand Jury" name made it all seem more intense, if that were even possible. He was convicted on three counts:

Count I: Kidnapping in the First Degree.
Count II: Sexual Abuse in the First Degree.
Count III: Sexual Abuse in the First Degree.

There was a lot more detailed information in the Grand Jury records. From what the court documents said, James had lured this little girl away from the day care center where he worked. That's why they accused him of kidnapping. *This just adds a whole new layer of creepiness on top of everything else.*

The other two counts were related to the sexual abuse he committed on this child. Count II was sexual contact by touching the vagina of a girl under the age of twelve years. Count III was sexual contact by touching the breasts of a girl under the age of twelve years. He was placed on five years' probation, with ninety days to be spent in a restitution center. He was also ordered to pay his victim the sum of five thousand dollars to cover her counseling. There were also mandatory orders to undergo and successfully complete "sex offender" evaluation/treatment at the direction of his probation officer. He was ordered to abstain from the use of intoxicants (alcohol, illegal drugs, or narcotics). He was ordered to also submit to breath or blood tests to determine blood alcohol content upon request, and submit to random urinalysis.

He was also ordered to take polygraph/penile plethysmograph examinations at the direction of his probation officer. He was to refrain from knowingly associating or contacting persons under the age of eighteen, including the victim. Lastly, he was not allowed to frequent where children congregate: parks, playgrounds, and schools, etc. Additional conditions were: Do not use or possess pornographic materials or any materials that may be used to foster sexually deviant interests. If all that wasn't enough, he's also not allowed to possess firearms.

Boy, I can really pick em'.

Wait a minute, I hadn't picked him at all. I was talked into dating him. I wish I'd listened to my gut. Never again will I ever let someone else talk me into something I intuitively knew not to do. There were many red flags that I ignored. I remember reading one of the psychological reports saying that he was a sociopath. Another report from a different analyst considered him a psychopath. However, I personally think he was both, a sociopath and a psychopath. He really lacked empathy and the ability to realize how wrong his actions were.

These people can be very convincing. They can be very good charmers, too, that's why other people like them so much. He certainly charmed everyone I worked with. *They ravish you, they give you all those compliments you've been so desperately craving.* Cut those ties immediately. The clear red flags I have learned *the hard way* are when they tell you the day after your first date how much they miss you, you're the love of their life, and I want to marry you, etc. James said all these things to me and then some. He also attached to me quickly. This is one huge red flag I, for one, will never forget.

What I do know for sure is how desperately I needed *and wanted* to stay away from this person. Legally he wasn't allowed to come near my daughter. That would be my excuse if I ever needed one. I refused to answer any of his calls. I think he got the hint pretty quickly that I'd been in the courtroom. On one of his voice messages he said he assumed I was there and the whole thing had freaked me out. *Well, duh!* He tried to convince me in another voicemail that he was talked into plea bargaining for a lesser charge, and with that he had to say he was guilty.

I call bullshit on that.

If I were accused of something this horrific, no way in hell would I ever say the word "guilty," especially if I were innocent. I had so much thinking to do, but I couldn't concentrate on anything. What the hell was I going to do now? First of all, how did my life take such a horrible turn in such a short period of time? Life happens sometimes and plays out like we are merely observers, watching it on a screen. I guess this must be what having no control over anything feels like. I remember feeling this when I was a child, but this is a big grown-up problem, and I have nobody to help me out of it.

However, what I do have is written in a stack of court documents on my kitchen table. I have the name and phone number of the victim's mother. I pondered for a long time whether or not to call her. What would her reaction be to the girlfriend of the monster who molested her little girl? Still, I needed more information, and especially the perspective from someone I somehow instinctively knew wouldn't lie to me. So I just grabbed the phone and dialed her number. She answered after the second ring.

"Hello?"

"Hello, my name is Julie, and..."

"You're James' girlfriend, right?"

I was completely caught off guard.

"Yes."

She was so kind to me, and right away told me she felt sorry for me.

"Oh no, I should be the one who's sorry. I just want you to know I had absolutely no idea."

She said she was glad I called but she also sensed I called for a good reason.

"Yes, I really need your help if you don't mind."

She told me the "incident" happened a couple years ago, and she's had time to deal with the horror of it all. She told me her daughter was doing well and still in counseling. *She must be a really good mother,* I remember thinking, *she's doing everything she can to help her daughter.* I was very surprised she would even give me the time of day. She was so reassuring and kind. Here I was, a horrible reminder of a terrifying experience in her child's life. However, she really made me feel like she wanted to help me. I think I subconsciously expected something different from her. It was reassuring to feel like I actually had an alliance in her. She put me at ease right away with her gentle voice and calm manner.

I went on to explain to her how I met James, how he manipulated my coworkers to convince me to go out with him, and how much I didn't want to date him in the beginning. She said, "Should've listened to your gut."

I was surprised to hear her use that term.

"I couldn't agree more."

I told her I didn't know about the court hearing until the day before.

"He waited until the day before his trial to tell you?"

"Yes, I was in so much shock I had a hard time understanding what was going on."

"Yeah, I'm sure," she replied in her very Spanish accent. "That was probably his plan all along."

She asked me if that was me sitting in the back of the room, and I said yes it was. She went on to tell me that James worked at the daycare center she took her little girl to. He had charmed everyone there, and he actually got the job by befriending the owners first. She seemed to know way more about him than she should from just being an employee of a daycare center. I felt so horrified as she continued. She explained how he instantly took a liking to her daughter. She said that made her a little uncomfortable, and like me, others convinced her that he was completely harmless. James had even requested for permission to take her daughter off the premises of the daycare, but she said no every time. *No every time?*

"Where was he wanting to take her?" I asked.

"Just out for breakfast, stuff like that."

"He always asked if he could take my daughter out for breakfast, too." *Sick bastard.*

I mean, of course it sounds innocent enough, but he was in the process of grooming his victims, me included. She said she was contemplating taking her daughter to another daycare because he was beginning to make her uncomfortable. She said the day she decided to leave the daycare was the day her daughter told her what'd happened. The bastard still found ways to molest her innocent daughter, ways to get her alone to molest her, multiple times, unfortunately. Even without permission.

I wanted to throw up. It was so disturbing to hear her talk about a grown man trying to have sexual relations with a child. I expressed my deepest condolences to her.

Then she asked me the million-dollar question: "Are you still with James?"

"No way, of course not, but I have a problem. I found out the day before he told me about his court date that I was pregnant with his child."

I could actually hear her gasp on the other end of the phone.

Without taking another breath she said, "You have to get rid of that baby."

"Why would you say something like that?"

"Because he will always have rights to the child. No matter what, he will have access to molest your child. He probably got you pregnant on purpose so he would have a child he could easily molest."

Considering my past experiences with my ex-husband, I really had to consider the validity of what she was saying to me. My ex abducted our daughter for an entire week following one of his weekend visitations.

He was scheduled to bring her back home by 6:00 pm on Sunday, but instead, he called me to tell me he wasn't bringing her back and I was never going to see her again. I remember when he hung up the phone my entire body sunk to the floor. I was scared to death that he meant it and I had no idea where she was. He even called every single day to remind me that I was never going to see her again. Even though I could hear her in the background crying and asking to talk to mommy, he wouldn't let her come to the phone. I pleaded and begged him to bring her home and all he did was laugh at me. It was the worst psychological torture I had ever experienced. He wasn't just torturing me, he terrorized my daughter, too. The courts didn't consider it an abduction because he was her biological father, he had rights. Regardless of the fact that he stole her and hid her out at his girlfriend's sister's house, he still had rights. The courts threatened me with contempt of court if I didn't continue to allow him his weekend visitations. One time, he even tied Stephanie to a bed so he and his girlfriend could go out to the bar, and he still didn't lose his parental rights. Shocking, but true. I seriously considered taking Stephanie and fleeing to another country far away. I never went through with it because I didn't want to live a life on the run. That wouldn't have been fair to Stephanie. If my ex could get away with all that, I'm sure it would have been a piece of cake for James to convince the courts that he was "cured" and give him full access. The thought made me cringe.

However, I don't believe in abortion. I was raised in a very strict Catholic home, and even though I don't consider myself Catholic anymore, the teachings are still very much a part of me. I believed having an abortion was a one-way ticket to hell. Aside from all that, I could never abort my own child. Not even an option in my mind. However, I had to consider what kind of life I was setting my child up for, too. This was just too much for me to even think about.

I told the victim's mother that it's my understanding our daughters resembled each other. She was shocked when I described what Stephanie looked like. She said our girls could be sisters.

"Sorry to have to tell you this, but James wasn't after you at all, he wanted your daughter."

No doubt in my mind now, she was completely right about everything. I thanked her for talking to me and said goodbye. She wished me luck and told me I could call her anytime. I never called her again. That was the most difficult phone conversation I've ever had. I felt that if I kept calling her, it would only bring back bad memories for her, and now it was time for her to let all this evil go and get on with her own life.

But now, what am I going to do about mine...

***

I think I need to gather more information. Is it true what she said about him having rights to his own child? Would the courts actually give a convicted child molester visitation? I had to find out for sure. Where do you go for this type of information? I decided to go back to his attorney. He wouldn't talk to me. Because the waiver was only for the documents, he couldn't talk to me about his client due to attorney-client privilege. Where do I go now? I decided to start with the District Attorney's office. I was able to find a woman who would talk to me "off the record." *I love how these people talk,* so I asked the big question....

"Yes, he would have rights."

What kind of screwy system is this? The same screwy system that kept giving my ex-husband rights, that's who. I wouldn't have believed it if I hadn't experienced it already. However, I can't ignore it anymore. I need to make a tough decision. I already knew what I had to do, but coming to terms with it was another thing. It was absolutely devastating to even think about.

Am I going to have to lose a child to save a child?

I can't wrap my head around this. There just had to be another way. I am so completely against abortion. When I was pregnant with my daughter, I was threatened by everyone I cared about ... everyone who I thought was supposed to care about me. They were all trying to talk me into getting an abortion. They said if I wouldn't agree to get an abortion, they were all going to leave me. My ex-husband even threatened me with physical violence in an attempt to make me lose my baby. My parents threatened to disown me if I refused to get an abortion. They also thought I should go live in a convent and give the baby up for adoption, or live with relatives far away. Still, I refused to get the abortion. How dare my parents threaten me when they were strict Catholics themselves, and raised me with the same beliefs.

I couldn't imagine, however, allowing my child the horror of being molested. I really need to get some guidance with this. I need to make an educated decision, not just based on one person's opinion.

Maybe I could give the baby up for adoption. However, the problem was, James already knew I was pregnant, and I would have to name the father. What if I went to another country and had the baby, and kept moving from time to time so James would never find me? That wouldn't be a fair life for my daughter. She has a family here. *Oh Jesus, what am I going to do?* How on earth am I going to face this?

I really should've listened to my gut. Look at all the trouble I'm in now. If all the hell I'd been through in my life has taught me anything, it's to listen to my own intuition above what everyone else is telling me. The problem is, I am not a confident person because of my abusive past. I have been abused and beaten down to the point that I barely have any self-esteem. My mother judged me for everything. Because I was beaten down both mentally and physically by my mother, I really lack confidence in myself. I was used to being told repeatedly everything I thought and felt was wrong. I was told so many times how to think, how to act and what to feel, to the point that I didn't even know how to think for myself. I'm still thinking like an abused person who judges and blames themselves.

Beating myself up now, however, wasn't going to solve anything.

But this wasn't about me, this was about the future of an innocent child. I needed some advice from people who really knew what the future could hold. I went back to try to talk to his attorney again. He couldn't tell me anything, no matter how desperate I was. All he would say was that he sympathized with me, and wouldn't want to be in my shoes. *Great, thanks, that helps a lot.* Where does a person go to get help with things like this? My next thought was the judicial system. The district attorney might know, but they were probably under the same restrictions as his attorney. My next move was to go to the police department.

I asked to speak to someone knowledgeable about child molesters. I told the girl at the front counter that I needed to speak with someone who could tell me whether or not they would have legal rights to their own children. She said she would try to find someone who could help me and asked me to take a seat in the waiting room. Finally, a man came out. As soon as my eyes met his, I knew who he was. He was the same person who came into the storage unit that afternoon when I was there alone with James. What a weird coincidence this was, that he would be the one person available to speak with me. I really don't believe in coincidences. I have had too many weird things happen in my life to prove otherwise. He looked at me and I knew right then, he recognized me, too.

"Aren't you the girl that was trying to hide when I came out to check on James at the storage unit?"

"Yes," I meekly responded.

"What can I help you with today?"

I blurted out, "I found out I was pregnant the day before James told me about his court hearing, which was taking place the very next day."

The look on his face said it all. He didn't even have to say a word for me to know how he felt.

"I'm so sorry. Are you ok?"

I lied and said, "Yes, but I need your guidance with something." I proceeded to explain everything to him.

In the middle of one of my sentences he said,

"Dear, do you realize he raped you?"

"Yes, I think I do, but we were dating and I let him stay overnight on my couch in my apartment and..."

"Did you say no?"

"Yes, repeatedly, and I tried to push him off of me but he wouldn't stop."

"You were raped."

Plain as anything, those were the words he said, *you were raped.* Why
am I such an idiot? Of course I was raped. *Again.* I think I just
couldn't bear the thought of having another rape attached to me.
How stupid I felt at that moment. I blamed myself for being raped.
I started to cry. All of the emotion of everything that had happened
came pouring out of me. The man I was talking to happened to be an
investigator that had been assigned to James' case. He was unusually
kind and comforting. I'd always pictured investigators to be stiff and
harsh, but not this one. He was very sympathetic to what I was going
through. Finally, I was able to pull myself back together. I got up
enough courage to ask him the most important question, the question
I came there to ask, the one question I desperately needed answered.

"Will James have parental rights to this baby?"

"Yes."

I never realized how one word could cut so deeply. *Just, yes.* Yes, this
child molester would have legal access to his own child. My worst
fears had just come true with one word. I had a million questions why,
but what did it really matter? The answer was yes, as long as James
completed all the counseling he was required to do, and as long as he
paid his debt to society. Society wouldn't protect his child from him,
because he was the biological father. At least, not according to the
laws of the State of Oregon at that moment in time. I knew what I
had to do. And, to answer my original question, it's a yes, too.

I will have to lose my child to save my child.

❧ 5 ❧

As far as I could see there was no place to hide, nobody to protect me or my child. He has rights. What about the molested four-year-old little girl who just had her entire life ruined? Where are her rights? Do people like this ever change? In my opinion, the answer to that question is no. It would be like taking someone who is naturally attracted to a man or a woman and counseling them to be attracted to a child. It just doesn't happen. You can't counsel the monster out of the person. They are going to be like this forever, and there's no magic wand or supreme counselor who's going to change this. Plus, there's the report that says he's likely to do it again, or quite possibly, even escalate.

This is life. *My life.* Stuck in the misery of something I never, ever considered doing. How could I go through with this? I am completely against abortion. I was going to go to hell if I aborted my baby. I was born to be a mother, not a murderer. In my opinion, abortion is murder. However, I have never been in this situation before. This is a horrible place to be. *The worst!* I will be condemned, not just by society and the religious high and mighty hypocrites out there, but by the spiritual world, too. I will be condemned to hell and tortured for all eternity.

Someone, please, help me get this Catholic crap out of my head.

I am still so brainwashed. This stuff gets engrained in who you are, that's for sure. How could God turn his back on me for saving a child from being molested? I knew if I kept this child, James would find a way to molest it. That was the whole reason he got me pregnant in the first place. I was raised Catholic and attended Catholic school for six years. I left Catholicism and became a Christian when I was twenty-one. Both religions agree about abortion, however, the Catholic faith is much more fire and brimstone harsh towards it. It's a sin, pure and simple.

However, the God I came to know when I became a Christian is much more loving and forgiving. Not someone to be feared, as I once believed. I was also abused in Catholic school. Now I refer to myself as a "recovering Catholic." I'm still a very spiritual person. However, I don't practice any religion, per se. I just got so sick and tired of the hypocrisy of it all. I am not better than anyone else who isn't a Christian. I don't automatically condemn someone to hell for not being saved. I believe none of us will know exactly what happens after we die until we are dead. Period.

What would Jesus do?

I'm not sure what Jesus would do, but I know what I have to do. Right now, though, I just really need someone to talk to. Someone I can trust to help me get me through all of this. The only person I feel I can trust right now is Mary

We've been through so much together and now, surprisingly, she's my best friend. I can't go to my parents with this. They would just judge me, plus it would give my mother all kinds of juicy new gossip to use against me. It's a pretty wild story how Mary and I ever ended up as friends. The deck was seriously stacked against us. I first met Mary a few years ago when she was hired to work in the emergency room. We came much closer to being mortal enemies. Mary had a very serious drinking problem that I wasn't aware of. She'd just started working the night shift with me in the emergency room, also as an admitting clerk.

We'd only known each other a short time, but I enjoyed hanging out with her at work. She was very funny and quite entertaining. Mary was reading the newspaper late one night at work when all of a sudden, she yelled out...

"I don't believe it! Quarterflash is performing at O'Callahan's this Friday night."

Who's Quarterflash?

"Hey Jules, why don't you come with me?"

"I don't know." *It wasn't like me to turn down an invitation to drink alcohol.*

Mary wouldn't take no for an answer and kept bugging me all night to go with her. I finally caved and accepted.

O'Callahan's was our town's most popular local bar and I really needed a fun night out. *This was a decision I would soon come to regret.* The minute we got there, Mary started ordering drinks. She didn't just order one drink at a time, like every other "normal" person I have ever gone out drinking with did. I'm not talking drinks like beer or wine either. I'm talking strong drinks like "top shelf" long islands. I've never seen anyone order multiple drinks for just themselves before. I've also never seen anyone drink them down as fast as she did. *She could really pound the drinks.* I remember telling her to slow down at one point. I was starting to worry about her. After about an hour, a couple guys walked up to our table and started talking with us. I really wasn't interested in talking to either one of them. One of the guys sat down with us at Mary's insistence. His name was Frank. I was a bit put off at the fact that we now had company. *Oh well, I guess I should be more flexible.*

Mary continued to drink heavily, then all of a sudden … Mary changed. She became aggressive, loud, and basically obnoxious. I guess I just wasn't drunk enough yet. I found her behavior incredibly annoying. Then, she leaned over to ask me if I wanted to go to the ladies' room and spilled her entire drink in my lap. By this time, I was pretty angry. Problem was, Mary could barely walk straight, so I asked Frank if he would help me get her to the bathroom. As soon as I got her inside the bathroom door, she threw up all over the floor and almost passed out in it. I barely managed to pull her back.

Not a pretty sight!

"Maybe I shouldn't have taken that medication."

I panicked and said, "You were pounding drinks after taking medication? You shouldn't mix alcohol and drugs, Mary! What the hell did you take?"

She wouldn't answer me.

I need to get this girl to a hospital.

Mary was almost completely out of it, so I asked Frank if he would help me get her to the car. I found her purse under our table and got her car keys out. Frank ended up having to carry her out of the bar. When we got to her car, she refused to let me drive. I told her, "There's no way in hell I'm letting you drive." While Mary and I stood there arguing in the dark parking lot, I could see Frank out of the corner of my eye trying to sneak away. Mary seized the moment and grabbed the car keys out of my hand.

Mary was a really small person, but amazingly strong. I couldn't handle her on my own. Luckily for me, Frank hadn't ventured too far. I called out to him for help and he ran back to her car.

"Frank, will you please help me get Mary in the car?"

He picked Mary up with ease, and sat her down in the passenger seat. Frank handed me the car keys. I quickly ran around to the other side of the car, sat down in the driver's seat and put the key in the ignition. Before I could even turn the key, Mary managed to pull it out of the ignition and threw it hard, right out the window. Then, Mary turned her small body sideways and proceeded to kick the hell out of me with her high heeled shoes.

I'm in hell.

"Goddamn it, Mary, I'm just trying to help you!"

I think by this time I was so pissed off at her, I was also threatening her with bodily harm.

"Mary, if you kick me again, I'm going to kick you back ten times harder." Mary didn't say a word to me in response which made me even angrier. *No apology, no nothing.* It was like she was possessed or something. She certainly didn't seem like herself anymore. I tried to get her to understand I was just trying to help her, but she wasn't hearing it. She got out of the car and started to run, but Frank managed to stop her, again. I was really grateful for Frank's help. I was a little concerned that I barely knew him, but at the moment, he was all I had. I couldn't have gotten her in the car without his help.

"Julie, how about I come along with you to the hospital to help keep Calamity Jane under control?"

"Yes please, get in."

We got Mary in the passenger seat *again*, and Frank jumped in the back seat behind her. He held onto her the whole way to the hospital to keep her from pulling the key out of the ignition again. That was all well and good, but it didn't keep her from kicking me in the side with her heels the entire way to the hospital. I screamed at her to stop, but she wouldn't. I just took it because it wasn't her.

I was afraid she was having some kind of psychotic break or something. She really needed emergency attention. I finally pulled into the hospital parking lot. Luckily for me there weren't any ambulances parked in the driveway. I was able to pull her car right up to the emergency room's back door. When I reached down to take the key out, Mary broke free from Frank's grasp. She grabbed my hand, pulled it to up her mouth, and before I could pull away, she bit down hard … right on the back side of my hand where it hurts the most. I remember thinking, "Oh great, now I'm going to be a patient, too."

It hurt like hell.

Frank quickly pulled Mary off me. I jumped out of the car, ran through the sliding glass doors and into the back of the hospital. I yelled for a nurse to come help me. We grabbed a gurney and headed back outside. In my attempt to get away from Mary, I didn't realize I no longer had her car keys. When she bit me, I probably dropped them. Mary must have done a great job convincing Frank to get her the hell out of there, because when the nurse and I came back outside, Mary was gone, along with Frank and her car. Now I was standing there, stranded and bleeding all over the hospital parking lot.

The throbbing pain in my hand was excruciating.

Who was I most concerned about now, me or Mary? Well, screw Mary, she's a crazy maniac who freaking bit me. I didn't know Frank at all, though. He seemed like a nice, helpful guy, but he could have been some deranged serial killer who just took off with my so-called friend. Well, I guess that was her choice. I needed to go back inside the hospital and deal with my bloody throbbing hand. Human bites are the worst kind to get. Even worse than any type of animal bite. Humans have the germiest mouths. *I'm so pissed off,* I thought. *This was supposed to be a fun relaxing evening, but here I am a patient at the hospital, instead. What the hell just happened to me? I better be more careful when I accept an invitation for a night out with someone I barely knew.* I got my shot and didn't say too much to anyone at the hospital about what happened. Mary was still a co-worker, and even though I was really angry, I was worried anything I said about her behavior could have gotten her fired. Regardless of what she had just put me through, I didn't want to be the reason she lost her job. I was a little worried about her, too, so when I finished getting six stitches in my hand, along with a few more shots that hurt like hell, I tried to call her. Of course, she never answered, so the next call I made was for a taxicab to come pick me up. There I was, it's two o'clock in the morning, I'm injured with a nice new hospital emergency room bill, and now I have to pay someone to take me home. You wait forever for a taxi to show up at two o'clock in the morning on a Friday night.

The next day, Mary's sister called me. *I didn't know she even had a sister.* Mary was too embarrassed to call me herself, so the big chicken had her sister call me instead. I told her sister what had happened and she didn't seem even a little bit surprised. She said she wished I'd known about Mary before going out with her. She also thanked me for not getting Mary fired. I told her about having to get six stitches and multiple shots, and she said, "Mary owes you big for that." " I agree, but do you think I will ever see the money?"

"Honestly, no."

It was really awkward the next time I saw Mary. I pulled no punches with her.

"Mary, I'm going to shoot it to you straight. You're an alcoholic with a serious drinking problem."

"I know, Julie, and I'm so sorry about what I did to you."

"Mary, you can make it up to me by paying me back for my hospital bill and the taxi I had to call to come pick me up."

"Of course, I promise."

I never believed I would see my money again. Money wasn't the most important issue here, either. I was more worried that Mary's life was in danger.

"Mary, tell you what ... I'd rather you pay me back by going to get some help. There's a meeting at the SOS club tonight, and I will go with you."

I took Mary to her first Alcoholics Anonymous meeting. The next day I took her to a treatment center an hour away from our town. I faithfully visited her when I could during their family visitation days. I wanted Mary to get as much support as possible. Mary was in treatment for a little over sixty days. She became very active in her sobriety, eventually sponsored others struggling with alcoholism, and even ran meetings herself. Mary and I grew to be very close friends through her sobriety.

I was so proud of Mary and all the work she did to get to where she ended up. I never gave up on Mary, and I was sure glad I didn't. Mary was a wonderful person. I got to know the real Mary, the sober Mary. Sober Mary was really a very kind, loving, and funny person. I'm going to support Mary in every way I can to keep her this way.

Now ... I desperately needed Mary to help me.

I called Mary and told her everything that happened.

"Mary, I'm going to get an abortion."

"Are you sure, Julie? Let's go get some coffee and talk about this."

After talking at length about what my options were, Mary agreed with me. We both cried over the prospect. She knew how much I loved children, how against abortion I was, and Mary knew how much this could destroy me. I asked her if she would take me to get the abortion and she said yes. The only place to go for one was in Portland, an hour away. I called, made an appointment, and we made the long, nerve-racking drive together. My emotions were all over the place. I could barely cope with what I was about to do. Mary and I never even spoke on the hour-long trip. I was too deep into my own thoughts to concentrate on anything else. When we arrived, Mary broke the silence and said "Do you still want to do this?" Since I'd battled inside my mind all the way up there with the same question, my answer was, "Yes."

I was barely counseled by a case worker, and then I signed the consent form. Then they do something so weird. They put this stuff that looks like leaves in your vagina and tell you to go have lunch and come back in a couple of hours. I don't remember what Mary and I did for two hours, other than walk around a store that sold Persian rugs. *I was a mess.* I couldn't possibly eat anything. What did they expect me to do? Go sit in a restaurant and pretend like it was just another day? What I was doing went against everything I believed in, but now the process had started, and there was no turning back.

I'd never felt pain like this before. The procedure felt like my insides were being vacuumed out. It was pure agony. I couldn't understand why they kept me awake for such a horribly painful procedure. Maybe they have to, I don't know. All I remember was screaming so loud I thought I was going to break all the windows in the building. Eventually they tied me down so I couldn't move. I still don't know why they tied me down.

Maybe it was for my own safety, all I know is it felt barbaric and gave me flashbacks of first grade all over again. *I was tied to my chair in first grade for being left handed. It was scary as hell.* I screamed, cried, and begged for it to stop. Nobody consoled me during the procedure, either. It was like a cattle call of one girl after another. It was horrifying. I never want to experience anything like that again. Under no circumstance will I ever put myself through that kind of trauma again.

Now comes the tough part, dealing with it.

After the procedure was over, they laid me on a cot in what they called their recovery room. It was basically just a corner on the other side of the room from where they were performing abortions. I just laid there listening to all the other girls screaming that were next in line.

How do people work here day after day? I couldn't imagine working there. The emergency room feels like a war zone sometimes, but this was a million times worse. I just laid there, all alone on a cot, recovering from the worst thing I'd ever been through. Nobody was there to help me. I started crying hysterically and became completely inconsolable. All of a sudden, and completely out of nowhere, a beautiful nurse with long, flowing, wavy red hair appeared next to me. She had the most beautiful hair I'd ever seen. It was so stunning to look at, I even stopped crying for a moment to tell her so. She also had the brightest and most beautiful green eyes I had ever seen. She almost glowed, she was so beautiful. She was acting like she was making the cot up next to me, but she really wasn't.

Eventually, she came over to me, put her hand on mine, and said, "You absolutely did the right thing."

"No, I didn't! I am going to go to hell for this." I was beyond hysterical. *I don't know if I really believed this, I was just distraught and out of my mind with the worst type of grief I've ever experienced.*

"That's just a bunch of religious crap they say to keep you scared." *I was a little taken back hearing her say that.*

"Jesus understands. You did the only thing you could to save your child. Your child will be taken care of, and eventually a loving family will raise him and he will grow up to do amazing things in this world."

Him?

"You, my dear, you're a hero. We know how difficult this was for you. You are blessed now because you did a very selfless thing. Your child was saved a horrible life. He would have been molested. Now, dry your eyes, my child, there will be peace when this is done."

How did she know?

***

And with that she walked away, and I stopped crying. It didn't even occur to me until later, the message in her words. I was in too much shock at the time to comprehend anything. Later, when I was getting ready to leave, I asked one of the other nurses where the beautiful nurse with long red hair was. I wanted to thank her for helping me to calm down.

"We don't have anyone working here who has red hair."

Later, I would come to realize, I had been visited by an angel. What other explanation could there be? I didn't tell anyone at the abortion clinic the reason for my abortion. The only other person who even knew was Mary. I asked her if she told anyone, and she completely denied it. She believes I was visited, too. I have had other experiences like this in my life, but they only happened during the most desperate times. They also only happened while I was dreaming, never when I was awake. There are mysteries in this world that I can't begin to explain, yet alone understand. All I can do is share my story as best I can.

Mary drove me home. I was exhausted and fell asleep on the couch the minute I sat down. The next day I woke up in extreme pain, nauseated, with a fever higher than I used to get when I had kidney infections. I called the clinic. They immediately ordered some antibiotics and told me to come up if it got any worse. I called Mary and she came right over.

Mary took one look at me and said, "We need to get you to the hospital, you look terrible."

This felt a little like history repeating itself.

I didn't want to go to the Emergency room where we both worked, I didn't want any of them to know I'd had an abortion, so we drove to the nearest town. We drove to a quaint little town called Silverton. They told me I had a dangerous infection. They couldn't believe how quickly the infection had spread, either. They said the abortion clinic didn't do the procedure right, and there were still what they called "retained products" left inside me that got infected. They told me I would need a D & C procedure, which is almost the same thing as getting another abortion. It's basically scraping the uterine lining (endometrium) with a spoon-shaped instrument to remove abnormal tissue. Luckily for me the doctor at the hospital took mercy on me and used a local anesthetic, so it wasn't nearly as painful. I was really grateful for that small favor. The hospital told me it was a good thing I came in when I did. I was in jeopardy of what they called "septic shock." Septic shock is also known as "sepsis," and it's when the blood becomes infected. It affects the internal organs, such as the kidneys, heart and lungs, which can immediately begin to fail. It can also cause dangerously low blood pressure. This is extremely life threatening. My body was already showing signs of sepsis. They put me on an aggressive medication regimen. If I hadn't gone into the hospital when I did, I bet I wouldn't be alive today. I probably came much closer to death than I even realized. It wouldn't have been the first time I almost died...

I remember hearing the word "sepsis" before, too.

Flashback to when I was fifteen and having another one of my kidney infections in a trauma room at the hospital. The last thing I remember hearing the nurse say besides the word sepsis was, "Doctor, we're losing her." All of a sudden, I could feel myself leaving my body. I rose up out of my body and floated upwards until I reached the ceiling in the corner of the room. I just hovered there while gently floating up and down in mid-air. I looked down at my body and watched while the doctor and nurses worked hard to save me. I wanted to reach down and make them stop. For the first time in days I wasn't in any pain anymore. It was incredible, and I don't remember feeling the least bit scared. *Not even a little bit.* It felt strange to look down and know that was me lying on the table below. That was pretty weird, but for the most part I didn't care, I felt great. It was very peaceful. There was no fear or panic of any kind, I was perfectly content to stay where I was. It was the closest I have ever come to experiencing the feeling of euphoria.

Seconds later, I felt hands on my back pushing me down with incredible force, until eventually I was back inside my body again. It was absolutely horrible and excruciatingly painful. It's hard to admit to anyone that I truly didn't want to come back. I felt warmth like never before, a pure sense of peace and contentment, and I was completely free from pain.

Why would I want to leave all that? However, I was only fifteen years old, and I still had a lot of life left to live. It was like I could almost hear someone or something in the distance telling me it wasn't my time. I blasted back into my body with such force. It was like slamming into a brick wall at maximum speed. When I tried to explain to the medical staff what had just happened to me, do you think any of them believed me? Hell no, it was the year 1975, and nobody had even heard of out-of-body experiences before. They said I was just hallucinating, but I knew the truth. I was healed up in the corner of that trauma room, no doubt in my mind. I could tell there was someone *or something* with me, too. I could feel them but I couldn't see them.

I was never afraid.

Eventually my doctor even admitted my recovery was nothing short of miraculous. Before I had my out-of-body experience, my doctor told me if my kidneys continued to fail, I would need to start dialysis. I might even need a kidney transplant. This was my future, until the night I left my body and experienced a miracle. However, I don't believe I was saved just so I could grow up and have an abortion. I really tore myself up over this for a long time. I'm sure others have judged me as well, but nobody could ever judge me more harshly than I judged myself. I'm sure this was the result from years of being abused as a child and growing up in a dysfunctional home.

I was sick for a really long time. Of course, I thought I was being punished for what I'd done. I committed a sin, and now I was paying the price. I went into a bit of a depression, too. I wasn't very stable after the abortion, mentally or physically. I can't explain what it does to a person to know they have a life inside of them, and instead of being happy and joyful, full of excitement and celebration, they go through a painful abortion instead. Don't let anybody fool you, abortions hurt. They hurt in every way you can imagine … mentally, physically and spiritually.

I was trying really hard to heal my body as well as my spirit, and I had no idea if or when I would ever recover. I never had the best self-esteem, so I probably didn't believe I deserved to feel better. I tried to remember what the nurse in the abortion clinic told me. *Was she a nurse or an angel?* It's going to take me a long time to grasp the message she gave me that day and forgive myself, if I ever do.

ᖰ **6** ᖱ

Now what should I tell James? I still hadn't talked to him. I never responded to any of his messages. I was avoiding him, hoping eventually he would just disappear. I also believed all my procrastinating was putting off the inevitable. Regardless of how I felt about him, I still thought the right thing to do was to tell him I wasn't pregnant anymore. However, what was I going to tell him? Should I be honest and tell him I had an abortion? Perhaps I should just avoid him. I kept going back to the fact that I really didn't know this person, and I was pretty sure he got me pregnant on purpose so he could have another victim. *Sick bastard.* I was extremely fearful of him now. I decided I would just have to tell him I had a miscarriage. I had the presence of mind at least to protect myself.

Self-preservation is also a strong motivator. At least I still had that going for me. I knew I couldn't tell him I had an abortion. Somewhere deep inside I knew I would be in a lot of danger if I admitted that to him. I knew he wouldn't take the information well and I feared he would be extremely angry. As I was working up the strength to call James, my phone rang.

I almost didn't answer the phone, but on the fourth ring, I answered it. I really wish I had gone with my first impulse and not answered it.

The person on the other end of the phone identified himself as Mike, a good friend of James'.

He was another person in the long line of people singing James' praise. It was sickening and disturbing. He really went overboard talking about James and what a great, almost perfectly angelic guy he was. *It was so bizarre.* According to everyone who claimed to really know James, they all thought he was such a catch. To me, James was just a very impressive con man. I knew there was a monster hiding inside. It's beyond my comprehension how he managed to fool everyone.

Mike told me he was married and lived in Washington State near the Canadian border. He also told me he and his wife had four children. He met James through work and they had known each other a little over four years. He said he would trust James explicitly with any or all of his four kids.

"Mike, do you know what James was accused of doing?"

"Yes, and it's all a bunch of crap, a big witch hunt. James would never hurt a child."

"Mike, listen to me, he took a plea bargain. I sat in the back of the court room during his hearing and clearly heard him say the word *guilty.*"

"He had to say he was guilty to take the plea. He would have spent way more time in prison if he didn't take the plea bargain."

"Did James ask you to call me?"

"Yes, because you won't respond to his phone calls, and that's just mean."

I couldn't believe he was calling me "mean." It seemed so childish to me at the time.

"Mike, I have a child the same age and the same characteristics as the young girl he's been convicted of molesting, how do you explain that?"

"So, you've made up your mind that James is guilty?"

"Yep, sure have."

"How dare you lay judgment on James like that? He doesn't deserve it. He's an innocent man."

Man, this guy is either really brainwashed or really stupid.

"Then he shouldn't have plead guilty."

Then Mike got really angry and yelled, "He plea bargained!!"

Same thing, stupid.

"Listen, Mike, if someone accused me of doing something I didn't do, I certainly wouldn't admit to it, especially if it's something as terrible as molesting a child."

I needed to get away from this character, and I was about to hang up when he said,

"What about the baby?"

"What about it?"

"Well, if you don't want it, my wife and I will take it."

His words felt like I was giving away a kitchen table or something. Seriously, who nonchalantly asks to take someone else's baby? All at once, it just came out, "I lost the baby."

Mike was silent for a moment, then he said, "I'm sorry, I'm sure it was all the stress of everything, are you OK?"

"No."

"Julie, you really need to talk to James."

"I was about to call him when you called me."

"Mike, I will call James, but before I hang up I really need to talk to you about some things I'm concerned about. You said you would feel perfectly comfortable leaving your children in James' care. You really need to rethink that. I can't explain everything I know, but please, if you hear nothing else I'm saying to you, please hear this and take it to heart. Never, ever leave your children alone with him. If you really love your kids, you will do everything in your power to keep them away from James. He's a monster, and you really don't know James at all."

Silence...

"Please, Mike, tell me you heard me at least. Please consider what I just told you. I know things you don't know about James. James is an extremely dangerous man. Protect your family from him Mike, please."

Click...

I know Mike wasn't listening. Either Mike didn't want to hear me, or something else was up. Perhaps there's more to all of this than I know. Maybe he knows lots more about James and doesn't care. How can you be a father of four children and continue being friends with a convicted pedophile? How could he continue to defend James the way he did? Didn't he know his kids would be in danger around James? Something about this didn't seem right to me.

I started to wonder how much I still didn't know. No doubt in my mind now that James was guilty as sin. I read those court documents and they scared the hell out of me. I'm probably the only one who'd read them besides the attorney and perhaps James, too. I really worried for the safety of Mike's children, even more so after talking to Mike. At least they lived far away in Washington State. Then I remembered James wasn't legally allowed around Mike's children. He was ordered by the court to stay away from all children. *At least there's that silver lining.*

James was a predator who had an uncanny knack of getting people to not only trust him, but to also speak highly of him, too. That's a scary combination, in my opinion. It was like his friend Mike idolized James like he was some kind of a celebrity or something. It was so totally strange. Mike wasn't the only one, either.

He really was the devil.

I called James later that day to tell him I had lost the baby. He was trying very hard to be sympathetic to me, but I knew he was getting angry. I could hear it in his voice. "I don't believe you, Julie." I'm sure he didn't believe a word I was saying, but I really needed him to. I was terrified of him. In my desperation I thought if I could start to cry, maybe he would believe me then. "James, why would I lie about something like this? You have no idea what this has done to me."

Those days it was very easy to cry. I cried most of the time. I was mourning the loss of a child in a weird sort of way. I think I was finally convincing enough, and when I sensed an opportunity, I quickly ended the conversation and got off the phone. I told him *in a very nice way* that I didn't think we could be together anymore, it was just too painful with everything that had happened. He agreed. *This was the last time I would ever talk to James.*

James now had bigger problems, like the prison sentence he would soon be facing. Talking to him brought up so many emotions for me. I never had a large amount of confidence, and because of my abusive childhood, I learned to doubt myself more than trust myself. I realized after hanging up the phone that I hadn't dealt with the trauma of finding out what James was accused of yet. *How did I feel about finding out?* First of all, the timing was so bizarre. The same day I find out I'm pregnant … I find out the father is accused of molesting a child. Then, the very next morning he goes to court and now he's a convicted child molester. It all happened so fast. How did I not see any signs? How was he so good at making everyone who met him instantly like him? I never met anyone who had a mean word to say about James. He was just a super great guy according to everyone he introduced me to. It would have been so easy for James to have convinced me he was an innocent man, had I not been so determined to get my hands on those legal documents. They really told a very disturbing story. *But was it the whole story? Is it finally over? Somewhere, deep down inside of me, I fear it's not.*

How does someone look at a child and get sexually aroused? After I witnessed the aftermath of an innocent child being brutally beaten and killed at the hands of his own parents, I said to the ER doctor, "I don't understand how people do some of the things they do." I found his response surprising.

"Be glad you don't. You'd have to think like them to understand why they do what they do."

How true that is, though. The only way to understand a killer is to think like a killer. The only way to understand a pedophile is something I will never know. However, I do know someone who counsels them. I couldn't possibly understand having a career like this, but I give great respect to those who do.

Can these people be cured? Can treatment and therapy really fix them?

I asked a friend of mine to help me answer these questions. She's an expert in her field and also counsels people like James. Even she's not sure if they can be cured or not. She said it all depends on the person. She did say that sometimes people are just born attracted to younger individuals. Sometimes they are abused and molested as children themselves. Then, when they grow up, they become molesters too and the cycle keeps repeating itself. The last thing she said was this, and I found it quite chilling. "Sometimes, there are just those people in the world who unknowingly or unintentionally give birth to monsters."

I have no answers as to why these things happen. It never made any sense to me, and it still doesn't. I guess you could look at it this way. *Not that I ever gave it any thought before James.* I'm attracted to men and I always have been. I could spend the rest of my life in counseling, but I really don't think any counselor, *no matter how good they are*, could ever make me attracted to women. I am just simply attracted to men, period.

That is how I look at pedophiles. They are just simply attracted to children. Regardless of how disgusting and horrifying it sounds, they are sexually attracted to children. I don't think they can be cured, and I don't think they should be allowed anywhere near children. Maybe some can control their urges, but what about the ones who can't? I think they should be exiled to an uninhabited island, or out in the middle of the desert. If it were up to me, I'd put them in the middle of nowhere where they can't hurt anyone, especially an innocent child. I know that's probably not possible, but it's certainly not reassuring to think they might be living in our neighborhoods, either. I wonder how many pedophiles are living near me at this exact moment. If you think too much about these things you wouldn't want to walk out your front door. I can't imagine anyone molesting my child. Honestly, I would find a way to kill them with my own bare hands.

It's a tough subject to talk about, and certainly one I didn't realize I had such intense feelings about. I've been through so much since meeting James, however, life goes on and I still have a daughter who is counting on me. I needed to pull myself back together for her sake. After about five years of struggling, I finally started to move on with my life. I was even starting to have some good times here and there. I was trying to enjoy life again. I was definitely on the right road back to being happy and living my life like I used to, before this all happened.

Or so I thought...

I didn't have any more contact with James after the day I lied and told him I lost the baby. He was the last person on the planet I wanted to talk to. As far as I knew, he was in custody and doing restitution. I went on with my life as best I could, not realizing how depressed I'd become. Getting back to my old way of life was hard. I was trying to fool myself into believing I was enjoying life again, but in reality I had very little joy in my life anymore. I did what I had to do, but other than that I was exhausted and sad. Having the abortion affected me much more than I realized. I never shared any of this with my daughter, she was too young. Throughout the years she knew something was bothering me, but I never talked to her about it until I was forced to.

One day I decided to share this with my counselor during another one of my many counseling sessions. She told me I hadn't really dealt with any of this yet. My counselor said, "If you were tough enough to survive it, you will be strong enough to write about it."

Here I am, putting all my hurt, suffering, and trauma out there for the world to see and for everyone to judge. But before I put a book out there, I really needed to have a private chat with Stephanie.

How do I tell her I aborted her sibling?

It took me about six months to find the right time. I don't know what I was so afraid of, she took it really well. I think since she was older, she could understand the heartbreak as well as the horrible dilemma I had to face. I think she believed me when I told her it was never my first choice, but I didn't feel I had another option. I was really glad I finally got my nerve up to tell her. I think it made us even closer. I was so afraid she would judge me and end up hating me for what I did. It was quite the opposite, and I realized in that moment, my daughter was healing my spirit. I really should have given her more credit. Stephanie is an amazing and very spiritually gifted girl. Stephanie and I have always been close. In fact, I think she took it better than most adults I've shared it with.

I've lost count how many times I felt judged for having an abortion. Most of the time it's the people who are "pure as the driven snow bible thumpers" who know they're perfect. I even had a "friend" tell me she couldn't be my friend anymore because of it. If I was still a member of the church and didn't already consider myself a "recovering Catholic," I'm sure I would have been excommunicated. I hate to admit it, but there have been times when I pointed out to the people whom I considered to be religious hypocrites ... that they are in fact, judgmental religious hypocrites. I know I should have just kept my big mouth shut but I was so angry, and it felt just a little bit wonderful getting all that pent-up Catholic school anger out.

❧ 7 ❧

Everyone has a story, and everyone has a past. Everyone has something they aren't proud of, some of us are just more open about our flaws than others. I'm very open about my ugly past with my mother. I never felt loved by her nor do I ever remember her telling me she loved me. I feel the need to be completely open and transparent about my mother because I sense I'm not alone. I know other people have lived a similar life to mine and who were also threatened into silence. Well, here I am, silent no more and it feels like freedom. I refer to my childhood as "an experiment in terror." My mother was an incredible piece of crazy work. I had a rough childhood because of it. I didn't know she had a mental illness growing up. When I tried to get closer to her it always backfired on me. I stopped letting my friends come inside our home after mom freaked out over me handing out a couple ice pops to my friends. I couldn't trust what she might do and I've been embarrassed too many times to risk it. I knew some friends who had parents that were alcoholics. They never let their friends in their homes either. Similar reasons but two entirely different illnesses. I remember a friend of mine who had a father who was an alcoholic. I felt so sorry for her but in total denial that I was in the same boat.

Moving on, back to mommy dearest.

My mother tried to trick me into having an abortion because I refused to get one on my own. I will never forget the day I told my parents I was pregnant. I drove over to their house to break the news in person. They completely freaked out. They took my car keys away from me, held me hostage in their home and gave me a three-hour lecture about what a slut I was. It was the most intense fight we have ever had. Because I wasn't married, my parents wanted me to get an abortion. They were only concerned with how it would make them look to their "high society" friends. *It really had nothing to do with me.* Because I refused to get an abortion, my parents stopped talking to me and basically disowned me. They turned their back on me for about three weeks. Then one day, my mother called and told me, "If you're going to keep the baby you should start seeing a good ob/gyn doctor." As usual, I forgave them and accepted her gesture. She set me up for an appointment with her own obstetrician. When the exam was over the doctor informed me that they didn't perform abortions in their office, they would have to send me to a clinic up in Portland for that. *I can't believe my mother tried to trick me.* I really should have had her arrested and charged with attempted murder. Luckily for me and my unborn child, her doctor didn't do abortions. I'm glad she assumed he did. *Joke's on you now, mother.* Imagine what could have happened if he did. He could have started the abortion process without me even knowing it. I was told by the doctor that once they start the process, they can't undo it. It would've been too late. Her doctor of over 30 years was so enraged by what she tried to do to me, he fired her on the spot. *Thank you, karma.*

What mattered most to my parents was their reputation, and how they were seen in the community. They were very much the "keep up with the Joneses" type of people. They considered themselves to be "high society" pillars of the community, even though they were anything but.

My abortion and many other aspects of our "not so perfect" life was never discussed with me or anyone else that I knew of. Especially not with any of their friends or family. This was intended to be kept quiet, nobody was supposed to know I got an abortion. It might tarnish their perfect reputation, heaven forbid. They cared about everyone around them, everyone except for their own stressed-out kid. It was all a mirage. My parents weren't loving towards me, especially not my mother. My father didn't do the abuse, but he certainly didn't do anything to stop it, either.

My second term in college I was brutally raped by a complete stranger who held a knife to my throat. It took me an entire year and a lot of prodding from close friends to tell my parents about it. I couldn't talk about it without crying. It even surprised me how emotional I was, I could barely get it out.

Who *wasn't* getting emotional about it? *My mother.* I think I saw my father wipe a tear away, but that was about it. Someone once told me, "When you can tell your story and it doesn't make you cry anymore, that is when you know you have healed." Obviously, I still haven't healed from my trauma yet, and I have my doubts I ever will. It was a brutal and terrifying attack. He told me, "I'm going to rape you, then I'm going to kill you." Luckily for me I managed enough strength to kick him right in the balls, grabbed my clothes, and got the hell away from him.

When I was finished telling my parents what happened, my mother looked at me, *more like glared at me,* and with the coldest expression she could muster up she said, "That never happened, you're lying."

Those were her exact words to me. Neither she, nor my father, ever spoke to me again about my rape. They never encouraged me to get counseling. They never gave me any kind of support, whatsoever. It was as if it never happened. It was "swept under the carpet." I wished like hell I had never told them. My father was always an enabler to my mother, an accessory to the crime, so to speak.

Over time I came to believe my father was afraid of my mother. Whenever I begged him to get her some mental help, he ignored me. She really did some strange things that would convince anyone she needed help. One night my mother went completely off the rails while my father stood by and did absolutely nothing. I had just returned home and mom was standing near the front door as if she were waiting for me to enter the house. In the entryway of our home stood a small end table against the wall, with an ornate gold framed mirror hanging above it. She looked at me and then motioned for me to look in the mirror with her. What horror waited for me, I had no way of knowing. Even though her request seemed odd to me, I stood behind her and looked in the mirror, like she asked. Mom was wearing her long purple velvet bathrobe that zipped all the way down the front. All at once she ripped it open while I stood behind her watching in horror what she was doing in the mirror. It was very strange how she only wanted me to see this in the mirror instead of facing me. Maybe that was the point, she wanted to make it as creepy as possible. As soon as she ripped open her bathrobe completely exposing herself, she said, "I'm going to scratch myself all over my chest until I bleed and then I'm going to tell everyone your father did this to me." *In horror I yelled,* "Dad, please get in here and make her stop." *This is exactly what my father did.* He walked into the entryway where she stood and calmly said, "I'm not impressed." Then he just turned and walked away like he'd seen it all before. *Seriously?* What exactly was he thinking by saying that? Did he want her to do something more intense to freak me out? I'm still not sure which thing freaked me out the most, seeing my mother's bare chest for the first time or the fact that she was abusing herself right in front of me. I ran up the stairs and closed myself off inside my bedroom. I grabbed my flowered suitcase and started throwing things inside. I could barely think straight but I had to get the hell out of there. I couldn't get the look in her eyes out of my head, either. As I packed my bag I couldn't stop thinking about how dark her eyes looked. It seemed that every time she freaked out on me her eyes turned completely black. I had to shake that thought for now and focus on getting my bag packed. I remembered some bathroom items I had forgotten, and zipped up my suitcase. I didn't have a clue where I was going to go but I knew I had to get the hell gone. I ran down the stairs and toward the front door. I didn't know where my parents were and I didn't care. I just needed to get away as fast as I could. As soon as I put my hand on the door handle, I felt my mother standing directly behind me. She grabbed my arm and spun me around until I was facing her. Then she started scratching the back of my hand with her long fingernails. In the distance I heard my father tell her to let me go. As soon as she let go of me, I ran. I jumped in my car as fast as I could and drove away. I still had no idea where I was going, but all that mattered to me was that I was finally out of there. I made my way to the freeway with blood dripping off the side of my hand and kept driving. I stopped when I got to a town two hours away from my home. I parked next to a gas station that was still open. I asked the gas attendant if I could take a nap in their parking lot and he said I could. I felt safer there than my own home and was able to fall asleep for a few hours. When I woke up reality hit me and I realized I still had nowhere to go. I'm just a kid with no money. I don't have a choice. The next day I went back home and nobody spoke a word to me about what had transpired the night before. It was never mentioned again. The sad part is, this wasn't my first time running away from home.

That, in a nutshell, is my mother…

❧ **8** ❧

I was still so terrified to have any kind of encounter with James. I changed my phone number and moved away from the dump we were living in. I stayed in the same town, but I did everything in my power to make it harder for James to find me. I was still working at the hospital because I was making good money by now, and almost had the hospital bills paid off. I feared someday he would walk back through those double glass doors. I wasn't as afraid of seeing him there, though. I felt pretty safe with all the security around me. Of course, when I found out that he was released early for good behavior, I obsessively looking over my shoulder everywhere I went. That faded a little over time, eventually things settled down, and life almost seemed normal again.

Until that one fateful evening....

***

It has taken me quite some time to build up enough courage to let this story out of my heart. And now, with every single word, I'm hopeful I can find a way to finally be free. It's a lot to carry something like this around. How do I tell people I'm still suffering because I chose to end a pregnancy? I certainly don't belong to any club of women who have tragically lost their child. Nobody wants to belong to that club. How does someone who lost a child have any empathy for someone like me? How do I not get judged for having an abortion? How do I not judge myself?

I believe it's me doing the most intense judging of myself. I fear the entire world will harshly judge me once the truth comes out. My intentions were pure even though the act was deliberate, violent, and some would even call it murder. It's occurred to me that perhaps I'm still trying to deal with it. All these years later it's also become clear to me that I have tucked it away somewhere very deep in my own psyche. The absolute truth is, I never, ever thought I would choose to have an abortion. It went against everything I believed in. I was raised in a very strict Catholic home, and to get an abortion is high up there on the charts of what sends you to hell. I harshly judged others who had abortions, too.

I have known girls who used abortion as their birth control method. Hard to believe, but it's true. I know of one girl who has had seven abortions. I could barely live through one, let alone seven. I have managed to convince myself all these years later that I had no choice. I had to have an abortion to save my child from a monster. Is that the truth, though? I guess I will leave it up to the world *and God* to decide.

There's so much trauma associated with all of this, too. I lost a boy-friend, who wasn't really anything worth crying about. Maybe it's the dream of what might have been that's worth mourning. None of it really felt real for a long time afterward, it all happened so fast. One day I find out I'm pregnant, and the next day I find out the father's a monster. Maybe it was just a really bad dream. But it wasn't a bad dream. Have you ever heard the phrase, "Real life is stranger than fiction?"

We all have our story that was written down long before we even arrived here on this planet. I have even been told that we agree to the life we will live prior to being born. It's all mapped out for us before we even get here. It's an interesting concept and I still have a tough time wrapping my head around it. I wonder sometimes, though, when I think about some people's lives, why would they ever agree to the horror they have had to endure.

However, I've also been told that our journeys lead us to something bigger and greater than ourselves, no matter how tragic or sad along the way. I know we are all here to learn and to grow as spiritual beings. Sometimes, though, I really wish my journey could have been a little bit easier and a whole lot gentler.

Just sayin' ...

One evening I was sitting in the living room, relaxing and watching a show on tv, when an alert came across the television. We don't get alerts very often so it really got my attention. Usually when we get them it's for thunder storms or an occasional Amber alert. I was hoping it wasn't an Amber Alert, but I wasn't at all prepared for what I was about to hear. *Nothing could have prepared me for this.*

The alert was for a man who was on the run and wanted by the FBI. I was surprised to hear when the alert said, "This fugitive is on the run and could be anywhere. He is armed and considered extremely dangerous. If you see this person, do not approach him, etc." I don't remember ever seeing an alert like this before. It went on to say this person is now on Oregon's top ten list of fugitives most wanted by the FBI. Who were they talking about? Who could possibly be this dangerous and wanted by the FBI that he ended up on my television alerting the entire state? Who could this possibly be?

James, of course...

I couldn't believe what I was hearing. It stunned me and I sat staring at the television in total disbelief. I don't understand how they considered him "extremely dangerous." Why was James considered so dangerous? There's got to be more to this story. Then my phone rang. It was Mary calling to ask if I saw the alert.

What the hell just happened?

"Mary, they said he was considered armed and dangerous."

"I know, Jules, are you alright? Do you want me to come over for a while and stay with you?"

"No, that's ok Mary, I'm fine."

"Julie, are you sure? I don't think you should be alone right now."

"I'm sure. Maybe come over sometime tomorrow, right now I just feel like I need to be alone." *I'm really bad at knowing what is best for me. I really shouldn't have been alone.*

And with that, Mary was gone.

I didn't understand why James was a top ten most wanted. Would this drama ever be over? I thought it was over. What I didn't know at the time was, the real drama was just beginning. I'd just started to pick my life back up again and was doing the best I could to move forward. *Now what?* Should I do anything, or just look over my shoulder for the rest of my life? What could I possibly do? Was there anyone I could call to get some advice about all this? Could I be in danger? What about my daughter, could she be in danger, too? A few days later, after some sleepless nights, I called the police station, told them who I was, and asked to talk to the detective. Unfortunately, he wasn't there anymore. He had just retired the month before.

"I will have the detective who took over for Detective Hamilton give you a call."

"That's ok, I don't need anyone to call me back." *Here I go, chickening out again. Or was I still feeling ashamed and embarrassed for having any connection to James?*

They replied, "You don't understand, we need to talk to you. Someone will be calling you shortly."

Great, now what?

I hope they call me back soon. It's going to drive me crazy until I know what's going on. I have a real talent for blowing things out of proportion the longer I am left to think about it. I have a flare for the dramatic, I guess you could say. I really have a great imagination for such things. Too bad I didn't make any of this up. How much simpler life could have been, *if this had all been just a dream.* Finally, I get the phone call I had been waiting for.

"Hello, is this Julie?"

"Yes."

"Hi Julie, this is Detective Clark, I'm sure you've been waiting for my call."

"Yes, I have, but I'm not really sure why you need to talk to me. Am

I in trouble or something?"

"Absolutely not." *He said with a question mark at the end.* He seemed a bit surprised at my trepidation.

"I have an important question to ask you, and if you need time to answer, that's fine. In fact, I encourage you to take a little time to think about it. It's a very important question. We need your help finding someone."

"Are you referring to James?"

"Yes."

"No. I want absolutely no part in any of this. You have no idea what this person has already put me through."

"If you're too afraid, or just don't want to get involved, we understand, however, we think you could be a big help to us. We really need to find him."

Against my better judgment.

"You really think I'd be able to help you?"

"Yes, we wouldn't have asked you if we didn't. In fact, I was against asking you because I understand he's really put you through a lot. However, he could be out there reoffending another child. We really need your assistance."

That's all I needed to hear.

"Of course. I'm terrified, but yes, I will help you."

"Great, we start tomorrow."

Tomorrow? I needed more time to get my head around this and prepare my mind for it. *I think I'm panicking again.* The best time for me to start would be the second Tuesday of next week. *As in, never.* I'm feeling scared right now, but I also think I need to do this. Not just to help them locate James, but for myself, too. I need to try to find a way to put this all behind me. Could this be more than just a person who didn't show up for a meeting with his parole officer? Duh, of course, there has to be more to it. They wouldn't involve a mere civilian like myself if it wasn't serious.

Detective Clark showed up right on time. He picked me up in an old, beat up, unmarked police car. It looked like something a grandmother would drive. You know, those gold cars all old people drive?

I see them everywhere in my neighborhood. I live in an apartment complex that's next to an assisted living facility and over fifty-five community. I'm not trying to mock old people, but they really do drive gold cars like Oldsmobile's or Buicks. They drive about ten miles an hour down the road, too, and I always get stuck behind them. Today was no exception.

"Is it always like this driving down River Road?"

Laughing, I said, "Usually is." This really helped me relax and it helped to break the ice.

"How did a nice girl like you ever get caught up with a guy like James?"

I was strangely flattered.

"He tricked a lot of people into believing he was a really good guy, and even though I didn't really want to go out with him, I broke under all the peer pressure."

Detective Joe went on to share some information with me he probably shouldn't have.

"We aren't just looking for him because he didn't show up to see his parole officer. He's a person of interest in a few unrelated investigations I'm working on."

I knew there was more to it.

Unrelated investigations, what could it possibly be? Could James have offended again? Could he be a suspect in a murder case? It seemed more likely to me that he molested a child again. Detective Clark wouldn't share any more than that, so I was left with my own wild imagination to guess what it was. Detective Clark told me he wanted me to know exactly what I was getting involved with. He said I could still back out if I wanted to. He assured me he would do everything he could to keep me safe, but nothing was guaranteed.

I was still putting myself in a dangerous situation. I didn't hesitate when I told him I would do it. This monster needs to be caught. Not just because he was a child molester, but now he could be involved in other crimes. Yes, I will risk it to get this monster locked up behind bars. I would have never imagined myself in this type of role, not ever. I'm just a girl who works as an admitting clerk at the hospital. Now I feel like I'm Nancy freaking Drew or something, and I kind of like it. Most of the time I was scared, but there were some enjoyable moments, too. I was really getting to know the detective, and he was genuine, kind, and just a great guy. I had sworn off all men, but I was starting to realize how unfair that was. You can't judge an entire race or an entire gender based on a few bad experiences.

A few really bad experiences.

I learned a lot from Detective Clark. He finally told me his first name is Joe. Detective Joe Clark. *It has a nice ring to it,* I remember thinking. He said I could call him Joe if I wanted to. He told me that pedophiles statistically offend 120 times before they are caught the first time. *120 times.* I had so many questions since I never had the bad luck of dealing with this kind of individual before. I asked Detective Joe if this was something people are born with or was it something they grow to become over time. Joe confirmed that usually they are victims themselves. Someone in their childhood molested them first.

This is heartbreaking to hear, and so tragic that this cycle continues to repeat. Just another disgusting cycle of abuse that isn't broken. Detective Joe said even though it's more common that molesters are victims themselves, sometimes people are born this way, too. Some people are just sexually aroused by children. These people are drawn to child pornography and masturbate to it until they become offenders. This was disgusting and difficult to hear, but very educational. I needed to know this stuff just for the mere fact that I'm a mother and I need to protect my daughter.

Knowledge is power.

Then I asked Detective Joe, "Can they be successfully rehabilitated?"

Detective Joe paused for a minute, then he said, "It depends. However, I don't believe many are successful at it."

Personally, I don't believe anymore that these people can be rehabilitated. They have something wrong in their brains. I've heard it referred to as a brain wiring issue, some kind of cognitive distortion or twisted thinking. Perhaps they can be successful at toning down or controlling the desire with enough work and intensive therapy, I don't know. I really have my doubts. This new information made the world such a scarier place to live in. But again, knowledge is power. I told myself not to be paranoid but to always be on alert. I used to think I already was, but evil still managed to creep into my life.

There are new programs out now, I've heard, that are there to help the abused child not turn into an abusive adult, and for those people who work in these areas, I applaud you. They are trying to get the cycle broken before they take the first step to offend. I pray more work is done in this area and someday, hopefully, the world can be free of this type of abuse. So many children would be saved if it were. More programs are needed, and more light shined on a subject most would rather leave hidden away in the dark.

I had no idea how much light I was about to shine on it…

You always think this kind of stuff happens to other people, until it happens to you. Even when it happened to me it still felt unreal. I've often wondered if James reoffended after I lost touch with him. I wouldn't be surprised to find out he had. I don't think he even gave therapy a try since he started missing appointments with his parole officer and didn't do any of the things they asked him to, *according to Detective Joe.* Joe told me James' parole officer ordered another lie detector test but James didn't show up for it. That is kind of proof right there he reoffended. That's what prompted the search, or that's as much as they were comfortable sharing with me. I'm betting there was way more to the story than I knew.

I think I'm about to find out.

I really was the best choice to help the detectives look for James. I accompanied him on so many of his home remodeling jobs. The scariest time for me was when we were driving out in the country looking for him. I'm not exactly sure why. Maybe it was because we were the only car on the road for miles, but I think it was because I felt so on edge. We drove for a while through windy country roads until we reached our first location. It was a mobile home out in the middle of nowhere. I thought this would be an excellent place for James to hide out. When we turned to make our way up the long gravel road towards the home, I started to feel myself freeze up. I could feel my heart racing and I started to panic.

I told Detective Joe, "I thought I could, but I just can't do this." I was just too afraid James would be there. Not only that, he was considered armed and dangerous.

Detective Joe told me I could just wait in the car while he went up to the door.

That idea didn't sound too good to me, either. I would be alone without any protection. What if someone snuck around the side of the car and ambushed me or something? I decided the safest place would be to stay with Joe. We walked up the long pathway to the front door, my heart beating harder with each step. I really respect the work these guys do, I would never be brave enough to be a police officer. I could barely make my feet move. We got to the front door and as soon as Detective Joe reached out to ring the doorbell, the door flung open.

"Get the hell off my property!" To my surprise Detective Joe remained completely calm and said, "Sir, we aren't here to cause you any trouble, we are looking for someone."

I didn't recognize the person at the door but he sure recognized me.

"You're that little lady who broke James' heart, aren't ya?" *I couldn't speak, and I might have just peed myself.*

Joe continued, "We are looking for James, is he here?"

"Nah, haven't seen old James since he was railroaded out of here by another angry woman."

What a freaking hick. Yeah, that's it, poor James…

I didn't believe him, and neither did Detective Joe. However, we didn't have any kind of search warrant, so we didn't have a choice other than to leave. I was so glad to get away from that place. We quietly drove down the gravel road, then to the dirt road, and finally made our way to the main highway. I was so glad to be away from there. I knew something was up with that old guy, and by the way … who the hell was he? I certainly don't remember ever meeting him. I could just imagine James was in another room in that trailer listening in on our conversation, and now he knew I was helping the detectives look for him. This thought scared the hell out of me.

Something just didn't feel right with that place and especially the old man who answered the door. I didn't know that hillbilly and I certainly don't remember meeting him. How did he know me? I kept getting this vibe that something was terribly wrong inside that mobile home. It will be interesting to see what happens with the other homes we plan to visit. There were a lot of them, too, our work was just beginning. Deep down, though, I feared something was strangely off with that trailer, I just hadn't figured it out yet.

Let the journey begin.

"Hold on a second, Joe, do you see that car in the bushes over there?"

Detective Joe pulled the car over and we both got out.

I ran over to the car and, sure enough, it was James' beat up old red work truck.

"What the heck is this thing doing out here?"

"Joe, that is James' truck."

Detective Joe got on his radio and phoned in our new discovery. I'm fearful James could be close by watching and would surely know I was helping the police look for him. Perhaps it's too easy for your mind to run wild at moments like this. *Especially my mind.* I was certainly developing a knack for it. Detective Joe and I decided to start walking through the fields and forest area near the abandoned car. I hadn't walked very far from the car when I stepped on something that appeared to be a passport.

It had a name on it I didn't recognize, but the face I did recognize. It was James' face on a fake passport. What the heck was this guy planning? Maybe he was ambushed and that's why his truck was hiding in the bushes on this backcountry road. Joe bagged the evidence, and we kept walking around until the investigators showed up. Joe explained everything we knew and gave them the evidence we'd uncovered so far. They were going to process the car for more evidence. Hopefully they would find some clues to help us locate where James was.

Joe said the car was most likely abandoned on purpose to throw law enforcement off his tracks. He said a lot of times fugitives will abandon their vehicles, then go to a bus station or fly to their next hideout, or better yet, find a way to get outside of the country. I bet he had more passports stashed away somewhere he could use. Why did he drop this one instead of his real one, though? If his intention was to make it look like he was in danger, wouldn't it have been better to leave his real passport? This didn't make sense to me. Now I was beginning to get a little worried about James. *Not a lot, though, just a little bit.* James was responsible for bringing trouble upon himself. Regardless, I am still a genuinely kind person, no matter what the situation. Perhaps too nice for my own good.

I mean, look at the mess I brought upon myself.

James ended up being a monster, but he wasn't a dumb monster. Those are the worst kind. *Smart monsters.* One more type of monster to add to my growing list. I have always thought that people who abuse children were monsters. Being from an abusive home, I had first-hand knowledge in this area because my mother was a monster. When it came time for me to start going to school, I attended our local Catholic grade school. I learned about a whole different type of monster in Catholic school. The monsters that hid there were the ones who liked to hide behind God in order to abuse innocent children. I used to think they were the worst kind of monster, until I met James. At this point in time, James took first place as the worst type of monster I'd ever come across. But that was about to change.

I was scared most of the time, but it was actually getting kind of exciting. It took my mind off of some of the anxiety and depression I had been suffering from. It really was a great diversion. I enjoyed the fact that I was really starting to think like a real detective, too. Maybe I should look into a new profession when this was over. I think I would be really good at it, that is, if I can overcome some of my fears.

The day was starting to come to an end and it was time to go home. Tomorrow was another day of searching. Every step we took seemed to open a new mystery into what happened to James. Did he really take off and run? Or was James himself in danger? This didn't feel like real life to me anymore. This was starting to feel like something out of a crime novel. However, who could make this stuff up? Who would even want to?

***

Detective Joe thought it best to stop coming to my home to pick me up for our investigations. I began meeting him at the police station just in case anyone happened to be watching us. It's a weird feeling, having to watch your back all the time. I was feeling very uneasy whenever I was out in public alone. It's quite an unnerving and unsettling feeling. There were times when I even felt like I was being watched. I felt somewhat safer at home, and that's where I stayed when I wasn't at work or helping Detective Joe. I'm convinced James still had his posse of supporters. How was I to know whether or not one of his supporters would be able to hunt me down at the drop of a hat? I never felt completely safe. Then again, why would any of them want to come after me? That was the real question. I still had a gut feeling I was in danger. I didn't want to believe it, but I can't deny it either. Look what happened to me when I ignored my intuition. I will never make that mistake again, *I hope.*

Truth is, I wasn't safe.

One evening I was watching television. My phone rang. I didn't get too alarmed, I had a secure unlisted phone number now. It was probably one of my girlfriends.

"Hello."

"Hello, is Julie there?"

"This is Julie."

All of a sudden, the voice changed from a normal person *sounded a bit like a girl's voice* to something that sounded like a computer-generated voice trying to imitate Darth Vader. *It totally freaked me out.* I sat there stunned, trying to listen to what the voice was saying.

"You are being watched. We know what you're doing and we don't appreciate it. We know where you live, we know where you work, we know who watches your daughter, and we obviously have your new secret telephone number. We know what you're doing at all times because we are always watching."

This is terrifying.

"You must stop your activities with the detective if you want you and your daughter to stay alive."

And then the phone went dead.

Once I could calm myself down and relax enough to get my thoughts together, my first thought was that it probably came from the idiots in Washington. They were crazy enough to still support him and do something like this. *But what if it wasn't?* How did they get my phone number? That had to have taken some skill. There weren't cell phones yet, and my number was securely unlisted. *The detective made sure of it.* To be able to penetrate a secure line like that, it must be someone or something else.

Who in the world was doing this, and why? Who was I angering, and why were they going to such great lengths trying to scare me? *It worked, I'm scared.* Maybe I wasn't just angering them, perhaps I'm more of a threat to them because I'm helping the police. But why would I be any kind of a threat? I'm just a regular girl who went out with the wrong guy. This was beginning to feel a lot more diabolical. Is it possible that this might not have anything to do with James? I'm wondering if this could be a lot bigger than just James being a wanted fugitive. By the way, *where is James?*

I have a strong feeling James isn't alive anymore. However, I found that really odd, too. Why would anyone other than the mother of the child he molested want to kill him? Who did I just talk to, and could this someone really be as dangerous as they wanted me to think they were? They had the ability to find my secure phone number, and that terrified me.

Who in the world was behind this?

I didn't care how late it was, Detective Joe said I could call him anytime if I ever needed anything. Now I desperately need something. *Security.* He quietly listened to me as I frantically rambled on and on, trying to get out what had just happened.

Detective Joe broke in and said, "I have just dispatched a patrol car to sit outside your apartment."

"Do you really think that's necessary?"

"Well, if someone has gone to the trouble of not just finding your phone number, but has the ability, *and the desire* to get their hands on the kind of technology required to disguise their voice in this manner, then yes, this could be very serious."

The question was, what lay person had the ability to get their hands on this kind of advanced technology? Maybe it was someone working for the CIA, or an undercover agent gone bad. *There goes my wild imagination again.* However, how was our little investigation big enough to produce such a thing, weren't we just looking for a fugitive? Just one guy who didn't show up to his appointment with his parole officer, *but oh yeah*, he's a person of interest in a couple other investigations, too. I really need to ask Detective Joe more about that.

One thing I knew for sure, these people aren't playin'...

I can't really explain what it feels like to know someone is watching your every move. It's a feeling beyond the violation one feels when they are burglarized. It's a deeper feeling than that. I've actually had someone follow me before. When I was dating someone my parents didn't approve of, they hired a private investigator to follow me. I felt completely violated. In fact, I was so angry at them I didn't speak to them again for over a year. I never knew why they didn't like the guy I was dating. He was someone my money-grubbing mother should have really approved of. He came from a very wealthy family and he would be inheriting an insurance company someday from his father.

My boyfriend's mother was actually the one who found out I was being followed. The man my parents hired to follow me also worked for their insurance company. He worked for them as an insurance investigator. When he found out it was their son I was dating, he felt it was a conflict of interest to follow me. So, first he fired my parents, and then went to my boyfriend's mother and told her everything. She was livid when she found out. *Talk about embarrassing.*

My relationship with the boyfriend ended soon after that. I don't blame him, I wouldn't want to marry someone who had parents as weird as mine, either. It makes me wonder if my parents even considered the fact that they hired a complete stranger to follow their daughter around.

Didn't they consider the fact that they might have been putting me in danger? *Probably not.* They only cared about how they looked to their high society friends. I was just in the way of them keeping up their facade of being high society, too.

However, this situation is different and it could actually be someone dangerous out to get me. How could I possibly keep helping the detectives after this? What would happen to me if I didn't back down? Was I putting my daughter in danger, too? *Was I really being watched?* I was going crazy wondering who it was that called me. Maybe it came from James himself. I doubt it, but it's possible. *I have such a battle going on in my head.* Am I brave enough to keep helping with the search, and more importantly, is it even worth it?

Maybe James really was watching us when we drove up to the secluded trailer in the woods that day. If he wasn't, I'm sure he knows by now I was there helping the detective. That is, if James is still alive and still in contact with these people. I wonder if he ditched his car on purpose not too far from the trailer to throw off the investigation. I ask myself … should I cave and let whoever this was threaten me and scare me away? I will give them this, they really did an excellent job of scaring the hell out of me. Am I really going to allow myself to be intimidated and bullied? Am I the kind of girl who runs at the first sign of trouble?

No, I am not.

I'm Nancy freaking Drew, and there's no way I'm letting anyone scare me away. Besides that, I'm a mother and I need to teach my daughter how to be strong and not back down to anyone, especially bullies who make threats. *Or, in my case, Darth Vader.* I absolutely will not back down. It might get me killed, but I believe it's always a good thing to do the right thing. I was becoming rather obsessed with moving forward. I was starting to feel like this was good vs. evil, and I knew that I had good on my side. I also knew that I was spiritually guided and protected. God wasn't going to let anything bad happen to me or my daughter. I had to believe that, especially now. I have divine help and that's all I need to keep this train powering on. Those idiots who made that phone call had better worry because I'm coming, and I'm bringing an army with me.

Exactly who were the idiots who made the "Darth Vader" phone call? I have my theories as to who I think it was. I strongly feel it came from that mental midget Mike, James' biggest supporter in Washington. The family man with four children who swore he would trust his children's lives in James' hands. *What a dumbass.* He gives me the willies. I can't say why, but I'm pretty sure he was behind it. I wouldn't be a bit surprised if he were hiding James out in his house. I hope Detective Joe doesn't want me to travel all the way up there with him. Hopefully, since I was never at their house, he won't. I didn't even want to meet these people. They lived up in Washington State in a little nowhere-ville town called Addie. It's up near the Canadian border, I've been told. I wouldn't be at all surprised if the phone call came from him. I still can't believe he tried to convince me to give him my unborn child. Who does that?
Creepy as hell…

It was so weird to look out my window and see a police car in front of my house, especially knowing that they were there to guard me. Now I know how it feels to be a celebrity. I don't ever want that kind of attention. It feels so unnatural to me. As I was looking out the window, my phone rang.

"Julie, how's it going?" *Detective Joe had such a soothing, calming voice.*

That seemed like a really loaded question today, with so much going on in my head.

"I think I'm ok at the moment. It's reassuring, albeit weird, to see a police car in front of my home."

"Julie, I think we are going to stop having you help us with the investigation. We are concerned that things are getting heated up and could be too dangerous for you. I know how uncomfortable you've been so far, and it's probably not a good idea to have you continue."

I thought about what Detective Joe said for about a second, and then I said, "I don't want my daughter to see me as a quitter. I believe I can still be of some service to you guys, and I would prefer to keep looking, if that's ok. I'm aware of the risks, but I have a strong feeling there's so much more to do, and I know I can still help."

"Well ok, Nancy Drew, if you're sure you want to continue, let's get back to it. Ready to meet me at the station in an hour and do some more digging?"

"Is that just a figure of speech or are we actually going to go digging somewhere?"

"I'm not sure, let's see where the day takes us."

"Hey Detective Joe, before I let you go, what exactly are the other investigations you're working on regarding James?"

"Well, Julie, I'm sorry but I can't share that information with you. I can only tell you he's a person of interest in a couple very important investigations."

Great...

Detective Joe, not just a pretty face, but funny, too. He had a really dry sense of humor and was a fun guy to hang out with. I'd already spent lots of time talking about life with him while riding around in his crappy old police car. If the situation had been different, I could actually see myself with Detective Joe. That would be crazy, and it's even crazier to think about.

I'm still recovering the loss of ... I don't even know what to call the pseudo-relationship I had with James. It wasn't even a real relationship. It was a huge mistake and now I think I was marked by him because I have a daughter. James wasn't interested in me at all. He was only after my child, and that was just too creepy to think about. However, I'm kind of liking Detective Joe. A relationship was the last thing in the world I needed right now.

Snap out of it, girl, you have work to do.

Detective Joe and I went back out in the woods where James' truck had been abandoned. We decided to keep looking around as much as we could while we still had daylight. There was a lot of ground to cover and every inch had to be carefully examined for things hiding in the grass or behind a bush.

As we walked together through the field into the forestry area I said, "Joe, what do you make of the fact that I found James' fake passport?

Is James running from the law or running from someone else?"

"Yes, I personally believe James is running from the law. We're still processing the truck and the passport for fingerprints, along with a few other things we found in the area."

"What else was found in the area?"

"I'm not at liberty to say, but I can tell you we are leaning toward being a little more concerned for James' well-being, even though I doubt that's the case."

Interesting, maybe James really didn't ditch his truck out here to throw off the police. Maybe there is another reason James went missing and didn't make it to his parole visits. This was getting intense. I'm starting to believe James really was in danger and we were all wrong thinking he just ignored court orders and took off. *I still think James is dead.* I was having a little trouble believing this scenario, though. Especially when I go back over in my mind all the documents I read in his lawyer's file. It's a battle in my own head, that's for sure.

It's not exactly logical that James would be innocent, but it's probable. Could he actually be an innocent man? He did plea bargain in front of the Grand Jury, and he swore up and down that he was innocent and only took a plea bargain because his lawyer told him it was the only option he had. *Could James actually be an innocent man, and I'm the bad guy who just terminated a pregnancy?*

Maybe he wasn't lying after all. Maybe he was in trouble since we found his truck out in the middle of nowhere along with his fake passport laying on the ground. Could I have been wrong about him all along? Maybe he was actually a victim. I know usually when cars are found they have been dumped because the owner is a victim of murder. I needed to get off this crazy train. I know better than not to trust my intuition so why am I questioning myself again?

My mind was going off the rails...

No way was he innocent. It wasn't just the lie detector reports I read that led me to believe his guilt, it was also the psychological evaluations from at least three different psychologists. It was all a bunch of pieces to a puzzle leading to one big concoction of guilt. It was a good thing

I tricked him into allowing me access to those papers. If it weren't for that I could have been easily convinced of his innocence. No way, nobody stands up in front of a judge and pleads guilty to something so heinous as molesting a child if they're innocent. All of these thoughts were running through my mind as we quietly searched the woods, careful not to ruin any evidence or alert anyone who could possibly be lurking nearby.

What the hell.

"Detective Joe!" *I couldn't believe how loud my voice just got.*
"Come over here, quick!"
"Joe, does that look like some kind of camera to you?"
"It sure in the hell does."

There was this shiny thing hanging on the side of a tree, anchored by the branches above, that vaguely resembled a camera. *Something's really off about this place.* I looked around and saw more weird things. I saw what looked like a crudely built old wooden shack a little further ahead from where the camera was. *This seems odd.* The camera was positioned in a direct line about thirty yards from where the shack stood. Why would anyone need a security camera for an old run-down, *most likely abandoned* shack like this? Joe quickly pulled the camera object off the tree, then motioned toward me to move away from the area. That was a relief, I can't get away from this place fast enough.

Joe motioned again for me to follow him without saying a word. I thought I was moving, but I was so freaked out I temporarily froze in place. I finally got my legs working and off we went. We moved away from the area and slowly toward the more heavily wooded area. Joe leaned in and whispered to me, "Follow me, as quiet and as fast as you can, just follow my lead and don't say a single word."

We slowly creeped along the path until we were hidden by the tall trees of the forest.
"I need to get us back to the car and call for backup," Joe whispered.

I couldn't speak. What the hell was up with this place? First the abandoned car that just happens to belong to James, then the discarded passport, and now a shack with cameras hanging from the trees.

"Joe, I don't feel safe coming out here again. There's something familiar with these woods, and I can't quite put my finger on it, but I feel like I've been here before and it's freaking me out." "That's ok, Julie, you've gone above and beyond for us, your work is done."

"Hey Joe, I didn't say I wanted to stop helping, I just can't come out here again, and I don't quite understand why I'm so freaked out by these woods. Why do these woods feel so scary and foreboding to me?"

And why do they feel so familiar?

Joe wondered if it was just because I had been out here with James before, and the memories were too hard to take, and I just needed more time to process everything. But it wasn't that, I had never been anywhere near this wooded area with James before. I had only been in the little trailer far away from the outskirts of the forest. Every corner we turned I knew what was coming next. That really freaked me out, too. It was like the most intense déjà vu I've ever had. That shanty run-down little shack in the middle of the trees? Somehow, I knew it was going to be there. *What's happening to me?* We are miles from where I live, and even further from where I grew up. How can this all feel so familiar to me? Not just familiar, but terrifying and creepy. The more I thought about it, the more it freaked me out, so I did my best to try and put it all out of my mind. I've had déjà vu before but nothing like this. Could I have been here before perhaps in a previous life? I've heard of past life regression or even having memories of a past life. I have no idea what's going on with me and this place. One thing I know for sure...

I know I've been here before.

9

Detective Joe and I continued with our investigation. *I wasn't about to quit now.* The police department has a name for what Detective Joe and I were doing. It's called, "knock and talk." I still wondered if James were in danger but I couldn't focus too much on that, we had a job to do, and that job was to find one of Oregon's top ten most wanted. Things seemed to be intensifying with each passing day.

So were my nightmares. *I was having the worst nightmares.* They felt exactly like my very vivid, almost real dreams, too. Maybe they were more like premonitions. When I look back, I realize we didn't understand the pure gravity of what we were about to uncover. We drove to our next destination with very little concern for what was coming next. *I guess ignorance truly is bliss.* Even though the strange dreams I was having lately were giving me clues into the future, I was still unable to put the pieces of this rather large puzzle together. We were coming close to uncovering the truth. The truth wasn't just about James. Surprisingly, it was about me as well.

How could any of this possibly involve me?

We traveled to a few more places, but instead of going to the door with the detective, I stayed in the car. It was getting too scary for me to go with him and James' posse didn't understand why I was there assisting the detectives in the first place. I was looked upon as a traitor. Detective Joe decided that I would be safer if I stayed in the car and out of sight. It took no effort for him to convince me, either. The anxiety it gave me just by walking up to their doors alone was overwhelming and I was much more content staying away, safely hidden inside the car. The people in every one of these homes creeped me out. They just gave me a creepy vibe. Maybe it was the weird way they looked at me, I don't know, but I think it was much more than that.

What I do know is, it was the exact same creepy feeling at each home we went to. Looking back, I recall I even mentioned it to James once. I told him I felt very uncomfortable around these people. He got offended and told me if I didn't like his friends then we shouldn't be together anymore. *Wait a minute, weren't these just people he did remodeling jobs for?* When I questioned him about it, he said he thought it was a good idea to build relationships with the people he worked for. Maybe that's why when we went to do a job on New Year's Day, we just sat around, drank beer and watched football. Regardless, it still felt strange and awkward to me. *And of course, there was that nagging familiarity.*

At one point in time, while we were just sitting around watching football, all the men quietly just got up and left the room. When I asked one of the ladies if she knew where they went, all she did was give me a blank stare. Then she got up and walked away, too. Finally, the group of men came back out, one after another. When I asked James why all the men disappeared, he kind of waved me away and said they were just doing some illegal gambling *in the back bedroom* on the football game.

You're being oddly dismissive, I don't buy it.

Why was James acting so weird around these men? Why wouldn't any of the ladies talk to me, and why wouldn't they let me in on what was going on? *What's really going on in that back bedroom is what I'm dying to find out. What's so damn interesting behind that door? I'm going to find a way to sneak back there and see for myself.* These women reminded me of an old movie I watched years ago called *The Stepford Wives.* The women in this movie weren't human at all. They were really robots created by the men of the town of Stepford.

The perfect subservient wives.

The real women I met on that strange New Year's Day were incredibly odd and robotic. It was so uncomfortable being around them at first. However, after a little time passed I couldn't stop thinking about these women. I couldn't shake the feeling that they might be in some type of danger and my fears only intensified over time. I couldn't put my finger on what the danger could possibly be, however, I couldn't stop thinking about them. I really struggled to forget everything about that day. I was desperate to get these strange people out of my head. I never made it back to the mysterious bedroom that day either. I tried to, but one of the men caught me sneaking around and stopped me from going inside. *I had to think fast and pretended like I just got lost looking for the bathroom.*

The women acted odd, but it was the men that intimidated and frightened me. They seemed very suspicious of me and kept a watchful eye on me the rest of the day. *It was a whole new level of creepy.* I didn't believe James's story for a second. I can only imagine what was going on in there, and my gut was telling me it wasn't anything good. *But why? What was behind that bedroom door?* Deep down I knew something sinister was, but what could it possibly be? What the hell was going on? *Damn, I wanted to get back there so badly.* I remember thinking, *Be careful what you wish for,* after we left the house. Maybe it was better for me not to know what was back there. My intuition was screaming at me to go to the police and report my concerns, but what could I possibly say to law enforcement? All I had to go on was a weird feeling.

They would laugh me out of the building.

Aside from the women acting strange, I also got a creepy vibe in the home itself, the same creepy vibe I felt in all the other houses James took me to. I'll say it again, these women were like human robots wandering around, doing what they were told. *Obedient, pretty, and polite, just like The Stepford Wives.* Were they drugged or something?

Oh hell, could they have all been drugged? These were just everyday housewives, or so they wanted me to think. Why was it all so mysterious, and why am I so suspicious? I feel like I'm getting some sort of message that I just can't piece together. Also, what the heck is up with my déjà vu lately? I keep feeling like I know these places, like I had been here before and ... even some of these people look at me as if I'm not a stranger to them at all.

One of the ladies at a different house hugged me like I was her long-lost puppy. I can't stop thinking that this is a lot bigger than I know right now, and I still can't shake the feeling that I absolutely know something. *Something bad, something evil.* What I did know for sure was, my subconscious mind was desperately trying to tell me something. This would turn out to be a huge clue for what was about to come. But, like I said before, I was completely oblivious to clues that were incredibly obvious. Part of me wondered if I was just being dramatic and making stuff up in my mind. Like I said before, I have a wild imagination.

Regardless, I hope I never see anything like that again.

***

Back in the real world I was relieved our investigation was finally nearing the end.

The detective and I pulled up to the last house James ever took me to on one of his "jobs" outside of town. It was at this moment I realized every residence James ever took me to was far away from the city, and completely isolated. Why hadn't this occurred to me before? Were all these homes connected to one another in some weird sort of way? Perhaps they all knew each other and had just referred James to one another for different jobs they needed done. *Sounds innocent enough.* I'm sure it's just my imagination running away with me again. I'm trying hard to convince myself I'm just imagining things even though there's something incredibly familiar and strange about this place. *There's that weird déjà vu feeling again.*

Yes, I'd been here before with James, but it was so much more than just that. It was more of a knowing I had been here before, as if I'd actually spent more time here or something. It was kind of like the feeling you get when returning to an old home you lived in years ago. Maybe I had lived here in a past life, that's how weird this was all starting to feel to me. I stayed in the car while Detective Joe went to the door. *I swear I just saw something moving near the back of the car.*

Maybe it was just someone walking by. I was probably just letting my fears get the better of me and causing me to be even more paranoid. *I've got to snap out of this.* My intuition suggested we were being watched, and it was getting stronger. I sensed this at every house we visited. People sense when they are being watched. I can't explain it, but it's just that feeling someone is watching you, and when you turn to look, no one is there. That's how it felt, over and over again. There must be something to it.

It wasn't just a feeling of people walking by a house, it was more like sensing people near the homes we were visiting and hiding in the trees, hiding in the woods. It was the sense that they were everywhere. I swear my imagination must be going crazy. Why in the world would anyone be following us and watching us? How would they even know where we were going to next? Truth is, we didn't know it at the time, but we really were being watched. Everywhere we went we were being followed *and we were being watched.*

The more I thought about it, the more I was convinced that every place I had visited with James was out in the middle of nowhere on purpose with absolutely nothing nearby, not even a barn or old farmhouse. *Not anything.* Just complete isolation. I believe it wasn't a coincidence that these homes were out in the middle of nowhere. *But why?* I still go back to that same old question, and I don't know if I will ever get an answer. What was going on with these homes? Other than some intense déjà vu and a few other weird feelings coming back to these locations, I don't have an answer, *not yet anyway.* This was the only house I actually remember James doing any *real* remodeling work of any kind at. Only one other place he took me to did he do any kind of work. He helped the owner replace a small section of wood trim, but other than that, we just hung out with the people who lived there. There seemed to always be an excuse as to why he wasn't able to work on anything when we got there. Either James didn't bring the right tools, or the supplies he needed for the job hadn't arrived yet.

While sitting in the car waiting for Detective Joe, I had time to really study the home. I noticed something reflective under one of the outside eaves near the garage door. I sat there and stared at it, trying to figure out what it was. It kind of looked like a flood light at first, but no, wait … it's starting to look a lot like that thing I saw hanging on the tree out in the woods. But these are just your everyday average residential homes. *Or were they?*

Why would regular people have surveillance cameras attached to their homes? It didn't make any sense. Now that I think about it, didn't I see other homes we visited recently with similar looking objects hanging discreetly near their garage doors, too? Why was it just now coming to my attention? Why hadn't I noticed this before? I bet that's exactly what that thing we took from the woods was, too, a surveillance camera. *They are most likely all surveillance cameras, but why?* Why would there be these cameras everywhere we just happened to be?

It almost felt like I was getting another weird vibe or an important message in a divine spiritual way or something. It's hard to explain, but things were starting to come to light for me in extremely random, tiny little bits and pieces. I was frustrated because I had so many questions but no answers.

I waited for Detective Joe to return to the car, and then I pointed out the shiny object to him. He found it curious, too, so he got out of the car to go check it out. It was both scary yet exciting watching Detective Joe at work. He was incredibly brave. I really admired him and his dedication to his work. What was I doing during all this? I was crouched down in the car, of course, hiding like a frightened little bird. This whole experience scared me in ways even I couldn't understand. I looked forward to the day it was over, even though I would really miss my chats with my unlikely new friend, Detective Joe. When Joe got back inside the car he said, "Looks like a camera to me."

"Joe, why didn't you take the camera off the house so you can see what's on it?"

"I would need to get a warrant first in order to do something like that. I can't just take something from someone's property without a warrant. There are rules in this business, Julie." *Stop rolling your eyes at me Joe.*

"OK, but what about the camera in the woods?"

"It was different in the woods because the recording was on the camera itself. The camera attached to the house most likely has film inside it. I could ask the people inside the house to give me their camera, but what do you think my chances would be of that happening?"

"Zero chance Detective Joe."

Joe and I were starting to get really close. I found him unusually easy to talk to, especially surprising because of the persona he puts out there. He is a very tall, extremely handsome, yet tough-looking cop who comes across as really intimidating with scary tattoos up and down his arms. He actually looked like he belonged in a tough biker gang instead of working for the police department as a detective.

I guess that look was the point, done on purpose because to do his job right and not get killed, he needed to fit in. I think he had no choice but to put that tough guy vibe out there because of his profession. I applaud anyone brave enough to do this job day in and day out because it sure wasn't for me. I really never got over being afraid each time I went out with the detective. "How do you do it Joe?"

"How do I do what?"

"This job ... day in and day out."

"That's a good question. I think I'm really just an adrenaline junkie."

"Yeah, I dated an adrenaline junkie like you before I met James."

"Lucky girl!"

"No, not really. He cheated on me. You're going to love this story Detective Joe. One night, shortly after we got engaged, he took me out to dinner and a movie. A short time after we got into bed together, he broke up with me."

I think dinner and the movie was my parting gift.

"Geez girl, you've been through so much."

"Detective Joe, you don't know the half of it, but I know a big secret about you. You're just a big softie with tattoos."

"Don't tell anyone Julie, I wouldn't want to tarnish my badass reputation."

The more I got to know Detective Joe Clark, the more I realized he was a really nice guy with a really big heart. Joe was a very sensitive and kind person who genuinely felt empathy for me and my situation.

"Julie, how did a nice girl like you ever get involved with these idiots?"

"It's a long story, Joe."

I really didn't want to talk about it anymore. I knew the answer to his question. It's because I was broken and broken people gravitate toward what they know, what they are familiar with ... other broken people. I had an abusive mother, so it was only natural that I would choose abusive boyfriends. Joe would have been a great choice for a boyfriend. He was really handsome and super kind to me. Unfortunately, I wasn't ready and this just wasn't our time. I think if things had been different, we would have made a really great couple. In this case, it just wasn't meant to be. Timing couldn't have been worse. I will always think of him fondly and I wish him the best because he deserves it. He's damn good people.

We were winding down our investigation, and I for one couldn't have been more relieved. I enjoyed spending time with Joe, but the work we were doing was getting to me. It was both scary and intense. I couldn't shake the feeling of impending doom, the feeling that we were about to uncover something we never could have imagined. Something way bigger than what we were looking for, something we couldn't see coming. But then again, I could be imagining all this, too.

It felt like we had searched the entire countryside when we were finally done looking for James. After we were finished, none of it felt normal. I couldn't ignore the nagging feeling that we were about to knock over a hornet's nest. *Why do I keep getting these strange vibes?* These vibes go way back to what I first felt from James when we met in the emergency room. This was a bit different though. I'm still getting the strange *and extremely* vivid dreams, but lately they are beginning to feel more like flashbacks from the past. In my dream, every person in every house was involved in something bad, something evil.

I've had lots of weird dreams throughout the years, and some I would even consider prophetic or psychically driven. *But this dream?* It felt like something so far out it couldn't possibly be a message or a repressed memory or anything other than just another one of my scary dreams.

Or could it? At this point in time it was a complete mystery to me. Maybe I was just getting too deeply involved with the investigation and it was playing tricks on my mind.

We still didn't have a clue where James was, and I really had my doubts if we would ever find him. I even worried we wouldn't find him alive. The question that keeps coming back to me is, why would he take off like that? He was done with his prison term and he only had to keep his life on the straight and narrow, keep the appointments with his parole officer, and stay away from children. Sounds easy enough to me, but then again, how would I know? I think back to what the ER doc told me; to really understand how someone thinks, you'd have to think like them. I don't want to come close to knowing how the mind of a child molester works.

The police were still busy processing his abandoned car, but they had just completed their search around the area where his passport was found. Nothing else was recovered.

Another dead end. This detective work is tedious, a little boring and when it's not boring us to death, it's creating way too much anxiety for my peace of mind. I often wondered if people in this profession were just adrenaline junkies. After spending time on this case, I really think they are. They live for making the world a safer place, but they also live for the chase and the excitement.

I went out to get my mail one morning, just like any other day when I dreaded going out to get my mail. I hated getting the mail so I usually waited until the mailbox was crammed full. My poor little mailman has even had to come knock on my door and personally hand me my mail. *Nice little subtle hint there from my mailman.* I would have hated me if I were him. I never got anything in my mailbox other than bills I couldn't afford to pay. They just piled up on the kitchen counter and I took care of the worst ones first. When they were about to turn off our electricity, that bill took priority over the rest. I had little tricks I'm sure they were all aware of, like sending in a check that I conveniently forgot to sign, or I "accidentally" mailed the phone bill to the gas company. I really struggled financially as a single mother. My deadbeat ex-husband was court ordered to pay me $250.00 per month for child support. I hadn't seen a penny from him in over a year.

However, today there was a dark brown, average looking package scrunched deep inside my mailbox. I never get packages in the mail so this was kind of exciting. I noticed there wasn't any postage stamped on the package. There wasn't a return address written on the package, either. It only had my name and my address written on the front. It also had the word "fragile" stamped with red ink on the package.

I think they were trying to make it look like it had been mailed and they wanted the postmen to take extra care with it. How could it have been mailed to me without any postage stamps or postage marks on the package. I was a little afraid to open it. I didn't know who it's from or what it could be. However, curiosity got the better of me so I opened it. Looking back, I should've taken more caution before opening it. I really should have called Detective Joe first. Too late, it's open now and I'm finding it a bit cool what's inside. Someone had sent me a VHS tape. I felt like I was inside a "Mission Impossible" episode where the recording says, "This tape will self-destruct in five seconds." Unfortunately, this isn't Hollywood and I'm not an actor. Part of me is still struggling with the fact that this is really happening. I don't know why but I always thought this stuff happens to other people, not me. It's silly to think that though when I look at how bizarre my life has already been up to this point.

After staring at the tape for a while and actually giving it some thought, I chose not to watch it alone. I decided to call Detective Joe. I will let him decide what to do with it and how best to handle this. He asked me if I could bring the tape down to the police station. He was still there, and they have all kinds of techy equipment we can use to watch it on. They might even be able to find out through their superior investigative methods where the tape came from.

Stephanie was already at her fathers for the weekend, so I got in the car and drove downtown to the police station. Even though I wasn't getting any child support from my ex, I didn't feel it was fair to not let Stephanie spend time with her father. I struggled financially and he knew it, but I never held it over his head, or used it as a weapon against him. I desperately wanted him to be a good father and involved in her life. Unfortunately, it never lasted long. He was a deadbeat in so many other ways.

I finally made my way to the police station. I must be anxious because it felt like it took a really long time to get there. Detective Joe met me at the door and I handed him the tape. I also brought the bag it was in to show him how it had arrived without any postage.

"Whoever sent this tape wants you to know, *they* know where you live."

Of course, that thought had already crossed my mind. How in the world did anyone know where I lived? After I broke up with James, I changed everything about my life, except for my name and my job. I got a different phone number and moved to a new location. It hadn't occurred to me to change my name, too. I'm not safe in my new place now and I will most likely have to move.

Where will I ever be safe again?

I was growing more and more apprehensive about watching the tape. Your mind does crazy things to you when you start imagining the worst. Why is it I instantly go negative instead of thinking positive things until I actually see what's on the tape? I think it's because negative is so much stronger than positive. To me it seemed like the obvious conclusion. I had no idea what was on the tape so why did I assume it was something bad? I was almost certain there was some kind of a threat on that tape and I was scared to death to watch it.

Detective Joe could sense my fear, so he offered to watch the tape alone. He didn't know what we were going to see on it, and it could be something horrible.

"No, it was mailed to me, I want to see what's on it."

"Ok, let's give it a go, shall we?"

"Yes, let's give it a go," trying to sound all brave even though my mind was screaming at me to run. I really was terrified to see what was recorded on this tape, but it was reassuring to have Joe there sitting next to me. When he turned it on, I didn't know what to expect.

Even though I had already gone dark and negative with my thoughts and had convinced myself that it was some kind of threat, what I saw wasn't anything I could have ever imagined. This wasn't terrifying at all, this was a confidant trying to help us. This was a very carefully disguised individual with good intentions to help us, not threaten us. They went to great measures to hide their identity. They wore a hooded sweatshirt and their face was completely blacked out. It still looked threatening and I had no way of knowing if this person was a man or a woman.

The most interesting part was how the voice had been enhanced. It reminded me of the phone call I got that sounded like Darth Vader. This was different, though. They weren't trying to sound scary like the phone voice was. They just didn't want to be recognized. Even though they went to great lengths to keep their identity secret, something about this person seemed familiar. *Again, with the weird vibes.* They were everywhere and getting more intense as I watched them speak. The footage was fuzzy and old looking. I remember wondering if that might be a clue in itself. The first word spoken by the mystery person was,

My name...

How the hell? Well, it's not so shocking, I guess, they knew where my mailbox was. This was the weirdest thing I've ever seen and I've seen some weird shit in my life. Somehow, I sensed it was a woman speaking on the tape, but it was so altered it was nearly impossible to distinguish. My intuition somehow knew, though. "Julie, please don't be afraid, we don't mean to scare you, we aren't here to harm you, we only want to help you."

Heavy sigh, this is almost a relief.

"We are the ones who have been watching you. I'm sure you have sensed it and many other things along the way. We had to find a way to warn you. You're in danger, and this is the safest way we could get a message to you. The people you are visiting are not good people. They are all part of the same cult." *The same cult?*

With these words the detective stopped the recorder. "Julie, do you know what we have here?" *No, not really.* "This could be something huge, or it could be a total hoax."

Just breathe…

"We'll have to do some forensic examinations on this tape and the package it came in to try to find out where it came from and hopefully, find out who produced it. We may never find out who's on this tape. It looks like they went to a lot of trouble to cover that up."

Detective Joe seemed to be getting a bit worked up. "This could be some kind of a religious cult or something … or they want us to think so just to throw us off our search for James."

"How could they know we were looking for James, though?" *This is getting really weird.*

"Ok, ok, detective, just turn the darn thing back on and let's keep watching." I was nervous but way more excited to see what was coming next.

The disguised person continued, "We need your help to uncover the horrible secrets that have been hidden in these homes for many years. Every house you have been to, we have been to. We were with you, following you to each house. Not only to follow you, but to help protect you if something went wrong. These are very dangerous people who have killed before."

Killed before? Killed who?

"Did you notice anything strange about these homes? Did you notice they all have surveillance cameras positioned on the outside of each and every house? This isn't a coincidence."

Well, I guess that saves us lots of time driving back by each one. I'm pretty sure Detective Joe will want to, though. We've already discussed the surveillance cameras. Maybe Detective Joe will get a warrant so he can examine what's on it. If what the person on the tape was saying is true, that gives them more credibility.

"We aren't the only ones watching you, some of the evil people in these homes are following you now, too." And then the disguised person said something that terrified me to my core.

"They desperately want you back."

Who wants me back? The freak shows from New Year's Day? *What the hell?* All of a sudden, my mind flashed back to New Year's Day. That was the strangest visit of all. I actually spent more time there than any other house, too. The women there were beyond odd. They moved in very strange and robotic ways and I don't remember any of them having a conversation with me. They would answer in one or two-word sentences but that was it.

What about the men? They were very scary and intimidating and they were all large with very muscular builds. Like a group of body builders or something. Why did the men go into one of the back bedrooms for nearly an hour? What was going on back there all that time? How could I be so blind? I believed the disguised person on the tape was telling the truth and desperately needed my help to uncover the secrets that were hidden inside these homes. But what in the world could that be? And what could it possibly have to do with James? He was only doing refinishing and carpentry work for these people. *Maybe that was just a coverup.* If it was a coverup, then why? Why was he bringing me along with him to these homes in the first place? I had a strange feeling this tape was going to leave us with many more questions than answers. I'm sure this had something to do with James but more importantly, what could it possibly have to do with me?

The mystery person continued.

"We heard that James went missing and then became one of the FBI's top ten most wanted. We were doing our own investigating near one of the homes when we saw you and the other man pull up. We had hidden microphones with us so we could hide from you yet still listen in on what was being said at the front door."

This must have been when I sensed someone near the car.

"James was a member of these groups and I, along with many others, were their victims. I managed to escape, along with a few other girls. We aren't alone … armed men broke into one of the homes recently to rescue us. They were also with us, so we could protect you too, if you ever needed it. We are still on the run, but we desperately need these people stopped. Not just for our sakes, but for the sake of our sisters and all the others that are still under their control and being held hostage against their will."

What the hell.

I'm quite shocked after hearing all of that and some of my own thoughts and fears are rising to the surface. It's going to take me a little time for it all to sink in. Could all my flashback dreams actually be memory glimpses from my own past? It's hard to imagine the enormity of what could possibly come next, and just how much this could change everything. Not just with the investigation, but with my own life. However, Detective Joe was still quite skeptical.

"Are you ok, Julie?"

"Yeah, just really quite shook up by what we just heard. What the hell is going on, do you have any thoughts on what it could be?"

Detective Joe was starting to look a bit shook up, too. "No, not at all, but don't worry, we will find out."

Oh great, another mystery to figure out. I still had a nagging question that hadn't been answered yet. This question had plagued me ever since we started driving around looking for James.

After watching this video, I just had to try again, "Joe, what is the real reason the FBI is so desperate to find James? I know it's not just because he missed an appointment with his parole officer. I mean, they want him so bad they made him one of Oregon's top ten most wanted."

Detective Joe kind of squirmed a little, and I could tell he really didn't want to answer my question. I know he was ordered not to say anything, but in light of these new circumstances, I strongly feel he needs to tell me.

"Joe, you have my word I won't tell anyone you told me. I just feel I have a right to know. I also feel you have an obligation to tell me since I've been risking my neck helping you."

Then Detective Joe said, "Do you remember when I told you at the beginning of our investigation that James was a person of interest in some of my other investigations?"

"Yes, I remember."

"The truth is, James is a person of interest in two separate murder cases I've been assigned to investigate."

Holy shit.

"Don't you think you at least owed me that little tiny tidbit of information before I agreed to help you look for him?"

Did I just risk my safety, *my life* to help them look for a suspected murderer? Now I know why I was never told. This information wasn't supposed to get out into the public because it could jeopardize the investigation. I really liked Detective Joe, but honestly, I would feel badly putting someone like me in a situation that could potentially be dangerous while risking my life by not telling me the entire story. *Guys ... sometimes think they know everything, I swear.*

"Did you really think that not telling me any of this was in my best interest? Maybe you didn't think I would help if I knew the truth, and you were desperate to find him. I understand I was the only one who knew where all these homes were located, but really?"

You owed it to me to tell me the truth.

I really don't want anything to do with this anymore. Good thing, since we are done with the "knock and talk" section of the investigation, and they probably don't need me anyway. At this point in time I doubt if I can be of any more help anyway. My big moment to get angry and quit was pretty much gone.

Detective Joe, in his cool calm manner, gently and easily smoothed things over. "I'm sorry Julie, I really should have told you, but I had my orders to keep that part strictly confidential."

***

I really wanted to be angry but it was hard to stay mad at him for long. Detective Joe really was just doing his job and doing what he was told to do. I wonder if it was hard on him, keeping me in the dark day after day. *I hope it was.* I hoped I mattered more to him than just a means to an end. I thought we had developed a really close friendship, but it puts a big wrinkle in the trust area when you know you've been kept in the dark. I felt like I had been lied to, even though I really hadn't. After I calmed down, I realized I really didn't have the right to be angry at Detective Joe. He was just following orders. He probably took a big chance telling me now. I will make sure I keep his secret safe. I don't want to get him in any trouble. But then again, I wonder if my anger really was justified.

Maybe I was just frustrated because I had no clue yet what was going on. I was especially haunted by what the person on the tape was telling me I know what they said, but was any of it true? Was this a cult, and if so, then what kind of cult was it? It sure didn't feel like it could be any kind of religious cult after meeting these people, albeit it briefly. They didn't give off the vibe of being religious fanatics. What in the world is this all about?

And where in the hell is James.

❧ **10** ❧

I decided to go a bit rogue and do some of my own investigating without telling Detective Joe. I don't know if that was a smart idea, but I desperately needed some answers. I probably could have spared myself a lot of hassle and just asked the detectives for this information, but I'm sure they wouldn't tell me anything. This entire investigation was considered "highly classified." Every time I asked them a question about whether or not James had gotten into any more trouble since his incarceration, they just shut me down. It was frustrating to say the least. I knew better than to even ask. I wanted to find out what James had been up to since we split. I know he spent most of it incarcerated, but there was a good amount of time, at least five years between then and now. I believed James was considered a high risk for reoffending because that's what it said in his psych evaluation. I wanted to get access to court records and I wanted to check on any current arrests he may have had since before he vanished. I started with the local newspaper. They had an archive department, and I decided that was the first place to look. What I found in those old papers completely blew my mind. It didn't take long for me to find a whole slew of information I had no knowledge of.

James had been leading a double life. James had been married three times before he met me, and was currently married to his fourth wife when he started stalking me at the hospital. *He was married!* Damn, I knew something was up with that jerk. I dug deeper. I got some real interesting stuff. Surprisingly, the information I got wasn't just about James, I found some interesting things out about his mother, too. His mother also had a police record of her own. She had been caught up in some kind of prostitution ring, and it was a huge bust back in the late fifties. It was definitely shocking to read this about her. She seemed like such a sweet little old lady. *She was also a very sickly little old lady.* She was much past her prime when I met her, so who knows what she was really like.

I remember James acted like he hated her, the vibe being in the room with the two of them was horrible. I never spent much time with them together after being in her little run-down house in felony flats that day. *Wait a minute … She lived in felony flats.* Felony flats is where many inmates from the Oregon State Penitentiary ended up living when they get out of prison. After more research it appears she did do some time in the Oregon State Women's Prison, which was located next to the Penitentiary back in the fifties. Thoughts, clues, and strange connections began flooding my mind. I guess it really does run in the family. *Runs in the family.*

Is this yet another clue? It has to be, because the hair on the back of my neck is standing straight up. There's got to be a connection. It's all lining up. How does it all connect is the big question, and an even bigger question is, how does it all connect back to me? I'm getting another one of my weird vibes, again.

Prostitution ring…cult activity.

That's got to be it. This isn't a religious cult at all. The person on the tape said they escaped with the help of other hostages, and they still needed to get their "sisters" out. This has got to have something to do with prostitution. But why, and most importantly, how is this all connected to all these different houses? How is it connected to James and now in the strangest way, James' mother. Could his mother be involved, too, somehow? No way, she's too old and feeble. I can't freaking believe James was married when he started dating me. *I mean, when James started stalking me.* Did his mother not know he was already married? She had to have known. She had to have been involved with whatever the hell was going on. His mother even tried to sell me on James just like everyone else did. *"Oh James, he's such a great guy, blah blah blah."* What a load of bull. She had to have been involved in his sick and twisted game. This was all an elaborate setup, and I was the target.

But the question still remains, *why?* Why is any of this happening to me? Why was I their target and for what reason? How could they all be such good liars? How was I completely oblivious to everything, including the fact that he was already married? There were just so many more questions now. *Will I ever know the truth?* Maybe the question now is, do I want to know the truth? What about the Washington contingent? Why were they always trying to sell me on him? They had to know he was married. *They had to have known.* Or, perhaps they didn't know. Maybe they were even bigger victims than anyone. It's getting hard to know who's a victim and who's the bad guy anymore. The lines are definitely getting blurred. Did the detectives know about this?

Not that I didn't already have too many unanswered questions, I just added a boatload more. I need to do more research. I went to our local police department first. I filled out the forms and paid the fee for a background check. All I got in return was a report listing a registration violation on a car. *Seriously, this was all they could find.* That seemed really strange to me. I wanted to ask them to go back and check again, but I didn't. Next, I went to the county police department. I filled out a form with his information on it, paid the fee, and again, waited for the report.

This report had absolutely nothing on it *but wait, is that his current address?* Holy hell, he still lives near me. James' most recent known address was less than five miles from where I lived. I actually had to remind myself that James was missing and probably not still living near me. I would have preferred he moved across the world from me. I had to shake this off and keep looking. My next stop was the Courthouse. I never found anything there other than the Grand Jury trial I was already aware of. *The one where I hid out in the back of the room and watched.* I talked to the clerk at the Courthouse, hoping to get some advice on where to go to next. We didn't even know if James was still in Oregon, so they referred me to the state police department to run another search. I went to the beautiful new Oregon State Police Department and they gave me a form to fill out to order a national search. I was instructed to fill the form out and then mail it to a different department.

When I got home and sat down to order the search, I couldn't believe what the fine print on the form said. Right at the very bottom in very small print the form stated that they would inform the person I was requesting the search on *and* let them know I was doing a background check on them. *Are they joking?* Why in the world would they do that? It also said they were legally bound to alert the person named in the search, which in my case was James. Would they really go tell James I was trying to get information on him? *I mean, if he were still around.* How in the world is that even close to a good idea? It certainly wouldn't keep me safe by any means. Why don't they just give him my address and phone number while they're at it? Plus, the realization that my own government enacted a law to make it legally binding really blew my mind. *Thanks a lot.* Needless to say, I never ordered that search. Thank God I read the small print. I mean, how many people don't?

I'm never going to get my answers.

I was so upset I decided to call the police department to get some clarity because I couldn't believe what I just read. I was hoping I could find a way around it because I really wanted to do a national search on James. I called and was put on hold by one lady, transferred by another, and finally spoke to a third person who took more time making sure I pronounced her name correctly. *Ok, now that that's out of the way, can we please talk about why I called?*

"I'm filling out the form to do a national background search on an individual. Is it true that you have to alert the person I'm investigating?" *I didn't bother telling her he was missing, I was just gathering information about their screwy system.*

"Yes, Ma'am."

"Is there any way you can do a search without telling him?"

"No, Ma'am. I don't have a choice, Ma'am. It's Oregon law, Ma'am."
Stop calling me Ma'am!
I was in shock when I said, "You legally have to send the information to that creep, letting him know I'm trying to dig up information on him?"
"Yes, but we won't give him your address."
Holy hell. On what planet or universe is this a good idea?
"Do you think it would be that hard to find my address?"
But wait, there's more.
I got the impression I was beginning to annoy the person I was talking to. She continued to tell me that not only would they tell him I was asking for information about him, they would also share whatever information they uncovered about him *with* him and give him the chance to agree or disagree with their findings.
What the hell is the point of that?

I don't believe it should be this big of a struggle to do a background check on someone, especially when they are already a convicted criminal who molested a child. Why would they protect the bad guy? Why is it that every time I try to get information on this guy I keep hitting brick walls? Why does it feel *again* like every place I turn to is protecting him? Even though James is currently missing and there's probably no chance he would know I was doing a search on him, I still can't bring myself to risk it.

I was an ancillary victim of his. I can't imagine how I would feel if I were the mother of the four-year-old child he molested. I think I would lose my shit on the entire ridiculous legal system. I didn't know there were different levels of sexual abusers, either. I was told if he wasn't a level three abuser it wasn't considered public information. *I disagree.* I should be able to get information about the creep without the creep being told. If someone molests a four-year-old, they should be considered a danger to society, and the police shouldn't be protecting them no matter how they decided to classify their crime.

How much worse could it possibly get? Maybe if he had raped or murdered her then I could find something. Perhaps, but they would still go blab to the monster who was requesting the background check. I will never understand it. It's unbelievable to me and I haven't been this frustrated in a very long time. I usually cry when I'm frustrated.

I could barely get through that conversation without crying.
"Goodbye, Ma'am."

It wasn't her fault she was following the stupid, stinky law our own government put out there. I have often thought I should run for office to try to fix these silly laws. However, I don't believe anyone would listen to me. I remember thinking when I hung up the phone, *now what, now what should I do?* It was such a struggle trying to find any amount of information. I don't think you can change the spots on these types of leopards. How is it possible I can't find anything else, all these years later? Only one charge for not registering a car? *No way.* Why does it feel like the police records department is protecting him from me? Why isn't his information public? It's injustice beyond frustration. I remember saying, "If you're that big of a dirt bag, you shouldn't have rights and protection."

It's like when I worked in the emergency room. I saw so many horrible things that never made it into the local newspapers. I was told it would create panic in the city if the public was told. It leads me to wonder. If we are only made aware of the worst of the worst, and they are the only ones making it on the news, what about all the others nobody knows about? What about all those other people, and exactly how many are there? It boggles my brain and gives me more to worry about. *Not that I need anything more to worry about.*

How bad do you have to be to be considered a level three sex offender in the eyes of the law? Molesting a child is damn high on my scale. It was so frustrating trying to get information on James, I finally just gave up. I was on a mission to answer my biggest question. *How does a child molester molest a child, and then just stops?* Unfortunately, I do believe it's more probable that he reoffended but never got caught.

That's one thing I do believe.

Now, even more than ever before, I want answers. *I need answers.* I feel like I'm on a mission, or perhaps I'm just too obsessed for my own good. I need to find a way to uncover the truth about these houses because if I know anything, it's that something's not right behind those doors. I know there's only one way left, and I'm even more determined to find out.

Now that I know I am destined to keep searching, I am going to have to go deeper with my investigation. I'm not going to share any of this with Detective Joe, and I'm definitely not going to tell him I'm still investigating. He wouldn't approve, plus they are too limited by policy to do any of the things I feel I need to do. But where do I go next? *That's actually the easy part.* I know what I need to do, and where I need to go. I'm going to find a way to get back into the mystery room at the New Year's Day house. *How am I going to manage that?*

I know, I'm going to stake the house out until nobody is there, and then I am finally getting through that bedroom door. *Even if it kills me.* The scary part is, it just might. Am I being reckless? This is real life, not a mystery or a detective movie. I really need some answers, though, and I am starting to realize this is the only way I'm going to get any. I'm intensely drawn back to that house and back to that room. What I can do is go hide out in the wooded area next to the house and just be patient and watch. I'm feeling very driven. Maybe even a bit spiritually guided. I'm not doing this just for myself, there's a much bigger picture here. I've never felt stronger about anything before in my life.

I think I saw an enclosed structure in one of the trees last time we were there, kind of like a hunting blind high up in a tree. I never liked those, but this time it's going to be very helpful. That's where I will hide. I also have a few skills nobody knows about that will come in very handy. I can crack open any safe or get through any type of lock or door around. My grandfather used to be a locksmith and I used to love to tag along with him on his work calls. I learned a lot of useful information working in his key store, and I have a feeling it will come in very handy for my next adventure. Especially if the doors to this home are all securely locked. I just need to remember to bring his tools with me.

I'm really feeling more and more convinced that I am doing something worthwhile, albeit secret. I'm surprisingly confident too. I'm beginning to channel my inner Nancy Drew and a brand-new adventure starts right after the holiday weekend. That will give me time to get a babysitter for Stephanie and plan my strategy. I wonder if it's the right decision not to share this with the detectives, though. I think for now I'm just going to keep it to myself. If anything comes up I will get them involved. I don't think they would let me do what I want to do, that's for sure.

I'm really not Nancy Drew, but thinking I am gives me strength.

My hands were shaking as I drove back to the creepy New Year's Eve house, except this time, I'm all alone and about to embark on my very first stakeout. What the hell do I know about how to do a stakeout? *This is crazy, this is definitely crazy. It's ok,* I kept telling myself, *everything will be ok.* I can just hide out in the deer blind and nobody will be the wiser. Nobody will even know I'm there. Oh crap, what if they have more of those cameras in the wooded area, just like they did in the other woods next to all the other homes out in the middle of God forsaken nowhere? *Stop.*

I will just take a little time to look around for cameras before I get started. I'm having some pretty intense second thoughts, and I can't believe I'm really going to go through with this. I should have told Detective Joe about my plan, but I doubt he would have signed off on it. No way would he allow it. I'm starting to doubt my plan and my confidence is fading. I'm really starting to freak out. What makes me think I'm even remotely capable of pulling this off. My self-doubt can be crippling at times. It's trying to sabotage me again. I need to stop doing this to myself. I'm just as capable as anyone else, maybe even more so. I'm feeling like I'm going to be sick. My heart is racing so fast. It feels like the closer I get to arriving at this location, the more intense my fears are growing, and I'm beginning to panic. That's it, I'm dangerously close to having a full-blown panic attack.

Just breathe…

This is the same feeling I used to get on the way to the beach when I had to drive past the exit to the crappy little dump of a town I lived in when I was married to my abusive ex-husband. For four years I couldn't drive anywhere near that exit without having a major panic attack. *I hate panic attacks. They always make me feel like I'm dying. Correction, it's a million times worse than that. They don't just make me feel like I'm dying. My panic attacks are so intense I believe I'm actually dying each time I have one.* Memories are strange that way, and time heals nothing. The town sucked, the house we lived in was a dangerous dump, not to mention I was eight months pregnant and my husband was cheating on me. The lights in the kitchen exploded almost daily and it was overrun with carpenter ants, rodents, and roaches. Every time I complained to our landlord, I ended up with an eviction notice taped to the front door. One evening the phone rang. The girl on the other end asked to speak to my husband. I asked her why she needed to talk to him and she said, "I met him at the bar last night and he gave me his phone number." *Tramp.*

"This is his wife and I'm a couple weeks away from giving birth to our first child." The really weird part was, she didn't care. All she said was, "Tell Steve I called." The best thing that ever happened to me was getting the hell away from that cheating bastard, that dump of a house, and that horrible little town. It's pretty amazing how I planned my escape, too. I even hid money in the freezer in case the fire trap we rented caught fire. I slept near Stephanie's crib so I could get her out first. I tricked him too into separating, then I met with an attorney the following day and got full custody of Stephanie. Yes, we do what we have to when we are desperate. Just like how I tricked James into signing the release form. When he found out I'd tricked him, he was beyond livid. I feared he might actually kill me this time. He broke down my apartment door, grabbed me around the neck and tried to throw me through my front window. When that didn't work, he picked me up again and held me upside down by my ankles. At that point in time I wasn't sure if he even knew what he was doing. He was pretty close to what I used to call, "blind rage." He'd never held me upside down by my ankles before but he tried to strangle me multiple times. I used to buy special makeup just to cover up the marks on my neck.

I had to think fast, so I told him, "There are two guys living upstairs who are professional body builders." *That got his attention.*

"I already told them all about you and your abuse. All I have to do is scream and they will come running. They are upstairs right now just waiting for my signal."

Funny how afraid abusive men are of other men. Especially if the other men have big muscles. He dropped me on my head and left. I had completely lied. There weren't any professional body builders living above me. I had just moved in so I had no idea who lived in the apartment above mine, if anybody. I just did what I had to, *to survive.* Later I found out that the upstairs apartment was vacant.

Ok, stop daydreaming and get back to the task at hand. At least it helped get my mind off my panic attack. I'm feeling better now and ready to get moving on this. It really takes some nerve to do what I'm about to do. I'm very aware of the danger, but miraculously, I'm managing to keep moving forward anyway. Whether it's a smart idea or a very stupid one, I feel very strongly that I must do this. I have to look deeper and find out what's inside that bedroom. It was like I was being driven by unseen forces to complete my mission. I can't explain it any other way. I am on a mission and somehow, I sense it's a very important one, too. *I've already survived a lot, I need to believe I will survive this, too.*

When I got there, I looked on every tree and under every bush. I was relieved when I didn't find any more cameras. Now I can safely climb the wooden steps up to the hunting enclosure. *Easier said than done.* It definitely didn't feel as sturdy as it first appeared, it was old and rickety. Most blinds are built on a stand. This one must be really old, because it's built on top of a tree branch with little support. The way to get to the blind was via a wooden ladder leaning against the tree. It was more like a tiny little treehouse. There was nothing secure or safe about this little structure. I climbed to the top of the steps and as I was starting to enter the enclosure, I found a camera. It was sitting right at the very top edge of the blind. I had to reach up pretty far to get it, but I managed to cut it off the stand without falling.

Luckily, I had some wire cutters in my locksmith tool kit to cut the wires that were supporting the camera. It looked like a surveillance camera at first, but now I think it's just a trail or hunting camera. Hopefully the police can find something on it that might help. But for now, business at hand. All I need to figure out is how to explain to them why I was there in the first place. *All in due time.* I will figure that out later, but for now, this is my only concern. Watching this house, staying out of sight, and, most importantly, staying alive.

Stakeouts are mainly just boring as hell. Sitting in one position for an extended amount of time can be extremely difficult. It's easy to forget to bring important items with you. Things like, toilet paper, food, water, and especially trash bags. Most of the time you're just sitting around, waiting and hoping for something to happen. It may sound exciting at first until you do it for a few hours, or worse, a few days. I really applaud anyone who can handle it over long periods of time. I certainly couldn't do it. I had a lot of time to think while sitting alone in that deer blind. What if you are doing a stakeout in front of someone's home, how do the professionals take care of their personal business? Luckily for me I was already out in the woods so I just had to wing it a bit, get inventive and hope that next leaf wasn't poisonous. I was always forgetting to bring the most important item, toilet paper.

However, going up and down that rickety old ladder was scary and probably more dangerous than I realized. I certainly didn't drink enough fluids during my stakeout days because I didn't want to have to pee very often. I also didn't want to have to take my eyes off the house, and I especially didn't want to go up and down those awful rickety steps. If I had been a guy it would have been so much easier. I could probably just pee in a bottle, but it's a lot harder for women to be successful with that. It didn't help that it was so hot and stuffy inside that wooden box, but I had to keep pressing on.

I don't know yet if I will ever make it into that back room, but I have to be patient, stay focused, and just do my best. Each day I was there, my mission became more and more of an obsession, but maybe it had to become an obsession to keep me coming back. It never once crossed my mind to quit. I'm a very tenacious person, too, so that probably helped me a lot. However, it was really my inner intuition that worked the magic to keep me moving toward getting the truth. I also had to be very careful to never leave any clues behind that would alert anyone to the fact that I had been there.

Every day I had to be very meticulous and careful with each detail to ensure I didn't leave behind any visible foot prints, food wrappers, water bottles, toilet paper, etc. I carried a plastic bag to take my garbage with me so not to leave any trace of my presence there. This got more and more difficult with each day, because being on high alert day after day was mentally exhausting. This was supposed to be a secret stakeout, and there were lots of things I had to be aware of. I couldn't risk anyone inside that trailer finding out I was spying on them. *I don't ever want to do anything like this again.*

I was there for over a week, every day, *all day*. Unfortunately, I couldn't see the back of the house from where I was perched, but I had an excellent view of the front. I really wished I had a better view of the back of the house, though. If I tried to move further in to see the back of the house I was certain I would've been spotted. I did see some movement in the back of the house, but even with my new high-powered binoculars, I still couldn't get close enough to see what it was.

It's so frustrating that I can't see the back side of the house. That's where the bedroom I'm dying to get to is located. I prefer to go in through the back of the house, *when and if I ever get the chance,* but there's only a sliding glass door back there, so my only other option is the front door. It shouldn't be too hard to get in through the old handle and lock they have on the front door. I hope they haven't installed a dead bolt since I was there. They didn't have one then, so hopefully they don't have one now.

There has been some questionable activity going on at the house these last couple of days. I found it very odd that I was starting to see many different semitrucks coming and going. As far as I know, nobody who lived there worked as a truck driver. The trucks were different ones, too, with different drivers, all of whom were men. Sometimes I even saw a girl or two get out of the truck with the driver. One time I saw a girl get out of the truck and the driver held onto her as if he was holding her up. I found that a bit creepy. Why would a young girl need help walking? I can understand why he would help her step down out of the truck, but the fact she could barely walk seemed questionable. Something was terribly wrong with this girl. I sensed she could barely walk because she was either drunk or drugged. Then, only a few minutes later the truck driver came out, got back in the truck and drove away. The girl stayed inside the house. This is incredibly weird. I have a feeling these truck drivers aren't good people. I think these girls are drugged and being held against their will. *But why?*

What is going on inside this freakshow of a home? *My curiosity is killing me.* I have to get inside this place. I'm dying for more answers, but for right now it's starting to get dark, and time to go through my meticulous routine of getting myself out of here and out of danger. I made it another day on this long and challenging stakeout. I don't know why, but I always felt the need to say a prayer for the girls that were inside this house before I left my sweaty perch. Not the truck drivers, or the people who own the home, but for the girls who were stuck inside.

I don't know if it's truly a home or not, it sure didn't feel like much of one to me. Were these girls all here on their own free will? Were they free to be here because they wanted to be, or was it just another clue to the mystery? I find it interesting, the word "free" in this context, and why would I be so concerned about them feeling free? I'm always free to come and go wherever I want to because this is America. Why have I always had such a weird vibe about these places and especially, *more importantly,* these girls. I also wonder if I should just go tell Detective Joe what I've uncovered so far. Do I have enough to go to the police with? I just worry I don't have enough evidence for them yet. I really need to find out more and I knew I had to get inside that house.

I've got to get to the bottom of this.

I'm going to take a much-needed day off. I could use a little break from all of this and have a little fun. It was opening weekend at the Oregon State Fair. I got some friends to come along with Stephanie and me for a little fun at the fair. I love going to the fair, mostly for the food. My favorites are pronto-pups and swirl fries. *Fair food is the best.* I also love elephant ears and cotton candy. I don't care much for the rides or the animal exhibits. I can't come near one of the stables without having an asthma attack, so I stay clear of those. Stephanie is also allergic to them.

We were just walking around, having a wonderful time, when all of a sudden my little group of friends came upon some of the people I recognized from inside one of the homes. They were actually staring at me *and my daughter*, and the way there were looking at my daughter really creeped me the hell out.

I was feeling extremely intimidated, and I think that was their intention all along. They walked by without saying a word to me, but the body language and the way they stared said it all. I made up some lame excuse to my friends, and Stephanie and I left the fair. Stephanie was a very good girl about leaving and it made me feel sorry for her because she shouldn't have had to leave. I don't know if I was acting rationally, but I think if anyone else had been in my shoes they might have done the same thing. I don't think my girlfriends believed me, especially one of them. That one girlfriend was Mary. She called me later that night to ask me the real reason why I left so abruptly. I made up a lie I hoped she would believe and got off the phone. I can't say anything to anyone and jeopardize what I am trying to do. But there's still that nagging question in the back of my mind. What exactly am I looking for, and what do I think I will find? I was also beginning to get a little suspicious of Mary. Maybe I'm just getting paranoid.

This is a hell of a way to spend a vacation.

I took vacation time from work to do this little spy operation of mine. I only have one week left to try to find out what's really going on inside that home. I really don't know what it is that's keeping me going, or if I even should keep moving forward with this. I keep thinking about that tape I got in my mailbox, but is that enough to risk my life over? Not just *my* life, what about my daughter's? Could I be jeopardizing her safety, too? What if it was all just a hoax? Should I go back to those woods and that horrible hot deer blind next week, or just quit now? *Stop!* I always do this. Psyche myself out with too darn many questions messing up my head. I think those people really got to me at the fair. I need to just put it all out of my mind, get my shit together and keep moving forward. I've come too far to quit now. However, I heard it's supposed to be close to one hundred degrees next week. That should make it extra fun inside that rickety sweat box. I really don't want to go back, but something is driving me forward. Some unseen force is telling me not to quit. My desire to get inside that house and keep pressing forward is growing more and more intense. *Almost like a divine calling.*

Good thing hunting season isn't in the summer. Nobody could stand to be outside in their hot camo clothes sitting in a sweat box. I want to burn that stupid deer blind down when this is over. I don't think it's fair to hide out like that and shoot an oblivious, innocent deer walking by. It feels like dirty pool to me. However, I have also said it's only fair that we arm the deer with guns to make it equally fair for them. *But how would they shoot them?* I guess I'm just not a hunter.

The following Monday I was back on the job. It was extremely hot out today, but somehow, I found the motivation to keep going. I brought a water bottle to pee in. I found out the hard way it's nearly impossible for girls to use them for that purpose. I wasn't there long when I saw yet another truck drive up and park in front of the house. I still can't quite fathom why there are so many trucks coming and going from this place. This time a man got out of the driver's side and went around to the back of the truck and let a girl out. Why wasn't she sitting up front with the driver? Who makes someone sit in the back with all the freight, and is that even safe?

I am at a disadvantage because I've never been inside a truck like this before and I have no idea how the back is set up. I have heard they have sleeping compartments, but I assumed those are closer to the front, not at the very back. A younger looking girl came out of the back, stumbled a bit, and almost fell down. She didn't appear to be very coherent. I bet she's been drugged too, just like I suspected with the other girl last week. This isn't looking at all normal to me, and my spidey senses are telling me I'm on to something. They were only inside the home for about thirty minutes when just the man came out, got back in the truck, and drove away. They never dropped off any freight, either. Something shady was definitely going on, no doubt in my mind. I can't keep trying to come up with innocent explanations for what my eyes are clearly seeing. There are definitely evil activities going on inside this place. It's doesn't look like a home to me anymore, it's more like a prison.

All I have seen are men drivers with a girl or two coming out of the trucks, and then they all go inside the house together. They usually aren't even inside for more than thirty minutes, either. This is the first time I have seen a male driver pull a girl out of the back, though.

Then, when the truck leaves, the only person I see leaving is just the driver and, every time, it's a man. Why, then, are trucks coming and leaving without the girl who came with them? I feel like I will lose my mind if I don't get some answers soon.

The next day, bright and early, while sitting in my sweat box I finally got a break. A moving van pulled up, and it appeared as if everyone inside the house walked out *like zombies,* one by one, and got inside the moving van. *This is just too weird.* This is my moment to finally get inside that house. I grabbed my tools, and I was so excited I almost fell out of the hunting blind. I was anxious to get inside that home and I knew I had to hurry. I was terrified, my heart was racing, yet I knew this could be my one and only chance to find out what was in that back bedroom.

I went to the front door, and as I looked at the door lock I spied a very tiny little thing next to the door trim. I instantly knew what it was. It was another camera. This one wasn't as big as the others and very easy to miss. It was painted the same color as the house, and if I hadn't gotten down to the level I was, I never would have seen it. I shudder to think of what could have happened to me if I hadn't pulled that tiny camera off of the house. They would have definitely known I was there, and that probably could have ended my investigation and quite possibly gotten me killed. I pulled that thing off the house and then proceeded to attempt to unlock the front door. I tried every tool I had and used every single trick I knew. I was trained by the best locksmith in the business, but I still couldn't get through that door. Again, it begs the question, what the hell is going on inside this house, and why the heck is it locked up like Fort Knox? Feeling very defeated I decided to go around to the back of the house, hoping there was some way I could get inside through the sliding glass door. I feared the odds of getting through that door were stacked against me.

As soon as I walked around the house, I noticed something back there I hadn't seen before. There was a rather large slab of concrete off the side of the house trying to look like a patio. It wasn't a patio, though, because it wasn't right off the sliding doors. There was a wood porch off the sliding doors, and this concrete slab didn't look like it belonged here at all. Why would this concrete slab be here? It appeared to be fairly newly poured, too. Maybe they are going to build a little patio and poured the concrete first, but it seemed really strange to me that it was in this position.

I can't slow myself down thinking about this, but it is definitely something I will need to share with the detectives. Right now, I just need to concentrate on getting inside this house and fast. The whole time I was hiding out I never had an opportunity like this and I can't waste it. I got back to the sliding door, and as I attempted to put my locksmith tool inside the space between the door and the hinge, the door moved a bit. At that moment I realized they had left the sliding door unlocked. They have Fort Knox in the front of the house, but they leave the back of the house unsecure and basically wide open. *Nice work Mensa's.* What a lucky break for me though. I slid the door open and quietly stepped inside the house. I quickly walked around, making sure I was completely alone.

Each corner I turned intensified my fear. I'm positive I saw everyone leave, however I'm terrified I'm going to run into someone in each room I check. The power of the mind is an incredible thing. I heard a car outside, and when I ran to look out the window, it was just some random car driving down the main road. I walked through the house as fast as I could. Now I can finally get inside that mysterious bedroom. As I approached the room I could feel my heart start to flutter. This is definitely above my abilities, and I can't believe I was brave enough to even attempt this. I'm very proud of myself for doing it. Some might call it reckless, however I believed it to be completely necessary. Now that I look back, I think my overwhelming desire to get inside that room ruled over everything else, including my own well-being. The intensity of my desire for answers was all I could think about.

***

I put my hand on the door handle, gently turned it, and walked inside. I was relieved when I didn't see anyone inside the room. However, what I saw there was incredibly shocking, and even more disturbing than I could have ever imagined. I could see multiple chains with handcuffs on the ends of the chains. These handcuff chains were anchored to the wall on each side of the bed. There was another pair of these shackles attached on the floor next to each side of the bed, as well as another pair hooked onto the bed frame itself. It looked like a torture device, or something I could imagine a dominatrix would possibly use.

Maybe the owners of the home are just into some kind of weird, kinky sex. I still can't wrap my head around what I'm seeing. I don't want to acknowledge what my mind is telling me. When things are too much, I think it is just human nature to try to minimize the reality of what's really going on. Especially when you can't wrap you head around what your eyes are seeing. That doesn't explain the random trucks coming and going with the girls, though. My gut is screaming out at me that something is terribly wrong here, and to get out. That's exactly what I did. I got the hell out of there, as soon as I took a few pictures to show the detectives, of course. I was shaking so hard I could barely hold the camera straight. I knew deep down what I had just uncovered was going to turn out to be another important clue.

Once outside I quickly walked around the house to take a closer look for more cameras. I think I'm starting to get paranoid. When I didn't find any more cameras, I hurried back to the hunting blind, gathered all of my things together as fast as I could, and got the hell out of there. I'm so happy I don't have to spend one more second inside that sweat box. I was very proud of what I'd just done, but I also had some intensifying fear that I couldn't quite shake. I was finally away from that house and safely back inside my car. I had to just sit there for a moment before I could even drive. I was feeling so shaky I barely had any strength in my legs, and my foot could barely push on the gas pedal. So I sat there for a moment, trying not to have another one of my panic attacks, and thought about what had just happened. First of all, I was finally able to get inside the house without anyone knowing. I found another very well-hidden camera by the front door and pulled it off the house, but most important … I finally got inside that mystery bedroom. I managed to get pictures of the weirdest bedroom in the history of bedrooms, so why am I feeling so much unease all of a sudden?

❧ 11 ❧

As I drove back to town I couldn't stop thinking about that slab of concrete. I definitely need to go straight to the police station and tell the detectives what I had found. It was just so out of place, and I'm sure it hadn't been there before. I guess they could be planning some remodeling or something, but my intuition told me to look deeper. It felt weird walking over it because it just didn't belong there. Why would someone pour a slab of concrete where there isn't even a door? It made no sense to me.

On a different note, I hope Detective Joe isn't too upset with me for doing what I just did. I knew I couldn't tell them because I was certain they wouldn't have allowed it. There was probably some rule in the department that would prohibit me from doing it or something. Hopefully, now that I have some great evidence for their investigation, they will let me off easy. I am so nervous driving away from the hell house, and I can't shake the feeling that I am being watched. *This is so unnerving* It was very scary what I just went through. I will just drive to the police station, and then I will finally feel safe.

I drove straight to the police station but was told Detective Joe was already gone for the day. Instead of involving someone else I decided to wait until Joe was available. I really wanted to share this with Detective Joe first so I decided to wait and went home to check on Stephanie. I feel so bad leaving her with a babysitter so much lately. I got to the apartments, and the first person I ran into was *of course* my stressed-out mailman. I had been neglecting getting my mail again. He hands me my stack of mail and I go inside my apartment.

Stephanie was very happy to see me. I told her we would spend much more time together but first thing in the morning mommy would have to pay a little visit to the detectives. I was very fortunate to have such a patient daughter. After I put her to bed for the night I decided I had better take a look at my mail. *Bills, bills, bills ... what's this?* Tucked inside the bills is another envelope with my name on it, but no postage. This time, however, it was a letter-sized envelope. I assumed it's probably from the same person, so I wasn't too afraid when I opened it. I opened the envelope and it was the most bizarre letter I had ever seen. It wasn't hand written, it was written with letters cut out from magazines. I guess she or he was worried I might find out who they are by their handwriting. I saw something like this in a scary movie once, but it feels extra creepy when it's in your own mail.

If you're wondering who this is from I will tell you. Yes, this message is from the same person who sent you the video tape. I'm assuming you've watched the tape by now, so I thought it was time to let you know a little bit about what you are investigating. I believe you are coming close to uncovering the truth. It's beyond anything you could have ever imagined. It's extremely dangerous. I already told you how I finally escaped, but now I need to tell you what I escaped from. This is a human trafficking ring. Not just grown adults, but children, too.

Human trafficking, really?

Every home you have been to, they are all connected. You are coming extremely close to uncovering the mystery ... their big secret of really being a massive cult, but it's not what you probably think. It's not a religious cult at all. They are all part of this huge human trafficking ring. They are all about trafficking young women and moving them from place to place.

They are also involved in child porn, child abuse and child moles-tation. This is so much bigger than you or anyone else could have ever imagined. I doubt the police even know that it's this big. You were a victim too, but that information will come to you later. At this time, you just need to understand what you are up against. This is every-thing you worried about and more. Your life could be in danger. You weren't intended to blow this wide open, however, you were just caught completely unaware in a Venus fly trap of sorts.

What's a Venus fly trap?

Now it's time for you to decide if you are brave enough to continue. You have our permission to take this information to the detectives.

Our permission? I thought this was just one person.

We are finally beginning to trust you, and even the detectives to some degree. I still must be careful not to expose who I am, especially now. I'm hoping you will understand everything someday. I wish you the best, stay safe, and God speed.

And with that, the letter ended. I knew this person or the group of people this person is with had been watching me in the past. I wonder if they still are and if they knew I was perched up inside the deer blind watching that house. I wouldn't be at all surprised if they were watching me, too. It almost gave me a feeling of peace to know that they might've been there as some form of back up to protect me. There is something very evil going on inside these homes, that I do know for sure. I should call Detective Joe but it's really late and I would probably wake him. I'm sure I will be alright to wait a few more hours.

I need to take my new letter and everything I managed to obtain from my undercover work to the detectives first thing in the morning. The camera from the deer blind, all the photos I took in that creepy back bedroom, the photos of the strange, newly poured concrete, and especially the videos of the trucks. I really think it is time for the detectives to get a search warrant and find out once and for all what's going on inside these homes.

More and more pieces to the puzzle are coming together. Is it true, what this person said on the tape and now in the letter? Could this really be a human trafficking ring? What did James really have to do with these people because I don't think he was just doing carpentry work anymore. I'm more than sure after reading this letter he had some kind of connection with them, and he was probably working for them in some completely disturbing way. How in the hell did I get involved with all of this? And most important...

What's the real connection to me?

That's a real concern that can keep a person up at night, and it certainly did me. What exactly is the connection to me? I'm also getting a strange vibe about James. At this point I would be very surprised if they found James alive. He had absolutely no reason for taking off. As far as I could tell, James was done doing his time and getting on with his life. There are just too many loose ends to all of this, and how can I possibly believe a person who won't even show their identity? *However, I really do believe them.* I have no reason not to and a million reasons to question James and the other freak-shows doing Lord knows what to innocent people inside these homes.

However, if what the person said on the tape and now this letter is true, then it's starting to make sense to me. The shackles in the bedroom, the cameras, but what about all those trucks? What's up with the trucks, and how is that all connected? Oh, and the strange women in that home. Maybe they really were all drugged. I still haven't figured out what the deal was with that shack in the middle of the woods. The placement of that shack was as strange as the placement of the cement slab. I'm desperate for the morning to come so I can get to the police station and tell the detectives about everything I've uncovered. I really wish I had more information on James, too. Thanks to the stupid laws in Oregon, I fear I never will.

It's finally morning and time to get to the police station. I'm extremely apprehensive now that it's almost time to go. I have no idea how mad Detective Joe is going to be that I went rogue behind his back. I'm just hoping the information I'm about to share with them will overshadow how I went about getting it. I walked into the detective's offices, and right in the middle of the hallway was none other than the person I was looking for, Detective Joe.

"Hey Detective Joe, how's it going?"

"Hey girl, what are you doing here?"

"Well, it's sort of an interesting story..."

"Julie, can you speed this up a bit, we are about to serve a warrant on that house with the camera."

"No kidding, well, that's exactly why I'm here."

"Ok, Julie, what did you do?"

"I just did a little something, something ... I guess you could call it my own little mini surveillance on the trailer home near the woods. You know, the one I called the New Year's Day home with all the zombie women inside. Just a little reconnaissance, that's all."

"That's all?" Detective Joe didn't look so happy to see me anymore.

"Who the hell gave you permission to go do that?" *I did.*

"Joe, before you get too angry with me, you really need to see what I discovered."

I proceeded to show him the photos and videos I had taken of all the trucks coming and going from the home, and then I showed him the photos from that back bedroom.

"What the hell is this?"

"Well, I think they are shackles. See where they aren't just coming off the wall but also off the headboard, the floor, and the foot of the bed, too?"

Detective Joe studied the photos and videos then he said, "Time to get another warrant."

They only had a warrant for the one home. The home where we first became aware of the surveillance cameras. They hadn't considered getting a warrant for the trailer but after the evidence I showed them, they were extremely interested in checking it out. The trailer wasn't far away from where we found James' abandoned truck. I wonder if there was a connection between the trailer and James' truck. I'm getting a strong feeling there is. I'm extremely suspicious of this place, more than any other house we investigated.

"Detective, there's one more thing I want to show you. Do you remember seeing this slab of cement in the backyard last time we were there?"

"Well, I never went into the backyard, but that definitely looks a bit suspicious. By the way, missy, how did you manage to get all these photos and videos of that place?"

"I just hung out inside a deer hunting blind up in a tree in the forest nearby."

Finally, Detective Joe began to laugh. "You've got to be kidding me, you climbed up that old rickety thing?"

"Yep."

"Unbelievable. I really should be angry at you for doing this, but I'm actually quite impressed. Aside from the fact that this was a really stupid idea and highly dangerous, not to mention you could have gotten yourself killed, is there anything else?"

"Yes, I got this letter in my mail yesterday."

Detective Joe got silent, looked a bit worried like he had seen this sort of thing before, or perhaps he was just in very deep thought.

"Those trucks could be transporting girls from one place to another."

That's exactly what I was thinking...

I couldn't stop thinking that I'm about to stir up another hornets' nest. More than likely, I probably already have. The messages I keep getting are blowing my mind. I'm being told that things I never could have imagined, actually exist. It would have so been much easier for me to believe that fairies and Bigfoot are real. Is this really a massive cult of prostitution, child pornography, child abuse, child molestation, and human trafficking? *Sounds more like slavery to me.* I used to think that slavery was dead a long time ago, but if all of this is truly happening, then slavery is very much still alive ... and thriving in ways none of us could have ever imagined. Could this really be much more diabolical than anyone suspected? The girl in the video and the recent letters tells me it is. I have so many questions flooding my mind. Is it possible that I'm the one who will finally uncover the truth?

How in the hell did I get involved with any of this crap in the first place?

I couldn't wait to see what the detectives uncovered at the first home. They had a warrant already signed by the judge, and they even called out the SWAT team to come back them up. Detective Joe assured me they were going to get a warrant to search the trailer home, too, but that would have to happen a bit later. I'm worried the evidence from the trailer would all disappear by the time they're finished with the warrant for the first house. All I can do now is try to relax and trust they know what they're doing. I am just so anxious to find out what's really going on inside these homes. I didn't hear from the detectives for about a week, but what happened in those few days was massive.

They got the second warrant. Now they can finally get inside to search that trailer. I was so relieved and desperately wanted to be there, but of course they couldn't allow it. This time I knew better than to try and push it. I just desperately wanted them to find out what's going on, there especially. What I didn't know is that they were also bringing in a cadaver dog to see if the dog could pick up anything under that slab of concrete. Perhaps the police think someone could be buried under there. *Interesting, that thought had never occurred to me.* What I hadn't had a chance to tell them yet was that I was still getting letters from my mystery informant. I hope they investigate that little shack out in the middle of the woods, too. I was getting a letter every day, and luckily for my mailman I was finally checking my mail every day, too. I got to where I couldn't wait for the mail to arrive, so I could see if I got another letter from my secret informant.

Those letters were getting stranger and stranger as time went on. They were still using magazines for cutting out the words instead of writing them by hand. However, as my mystery informant began to trust me, more and more information started flooding in. All my deepest fears were true, according to the informant. They insisted that this was a huge human trafficking ring and each time I got another letter, the enormity of it all grew even more.

Finally, the informant told me it wasn't just a local problem, it was a national and most likely a global enterprise. They told me if I were strong enough to keep moving forward, I could be instrumental in helping to bring down the largest human trafficking ring in history. This was starting to sound either extremely far-fetched, or there really is something to all of this. It was like how some things are too strange not to be true. That's exactly how it felt to me, how could anyone make this stuff up? What was my gut telling me? My gut was telling me that everything in those letters was true.

What a black mark on society if it were all true. However, the person who was giving me these letters really seemed desperate and wanted to help us. Whether any of it was true or not was yet to be seen. It was either a huge human trafficking ring or just a big hoax. It was difficult to believe, but impossible not to. I just wanted to get to the truth. I couldn't just pawn it all off as a lie. There's already too much information pointing the other direction.

What I wasn't at all prepared for was what happened during the search of the trailer home. Out of the blue I get a call from Detective Joe. He asked me if I had time to come down to the police station for a little impromptu meeting. He said he wanted to share with me what they discovered before I heard anything about it on the news. I rushed right down, wondering on the way what in the world they had uncovered. I couldn't have guessed in a million years what he was about to share with me.

"Julie, I don't know really how to tell you this, so I'm just going to say it. James is dead."

I couldn't even react or say a word at first, even though at some level I already knew. "Are you ok, Julie? Talk to me. I've never seen you at a loss for words before."

I think Detective Joe was legitimately concerned for me because it's so true, I really am rarely at a loss for words.

"Joe, how did you find out?"

"Well, we had a search warrant, not only for the trailer but also for that slab of concrete you showed us in the back yard. That concrete looked especially suspicious to us, so we brought in a cadaver dog to see if the dog could detect anything. The dog ran right to the slab of concrete and sat down. That is the sign the dog was trained to do if it detected anything. It means the dog smelled something near or below the concrete. Then we brought in a bulldozer and started to dig, and that's when we found James' body. The slab of concrete was newly poured there because they had recently buried James beneath it, hoping nobody would think to look there."

I'm so freaked out right now. I walked over that slab of concrete. I even stood on top of it. I had no idea James was under it, and it never would have occurred to me to even think that. I guess he's not a top Ten Most Wanted anymore. *This is so weird.* Who killed James, and why? Everything started to feel like it was moving way too fast. I think I need to sit down before I pass out. I'm getting really shaking and ... oh, I know what's happening, I'm having another panic attack.

"I think I need to sit down for a minute."

"There's more I need to tell you, if you're ready to listen."

I remember thinking I didn't want to know any more, but then again, I really needed to know more. I nodded my head and Detective Joe continued. I'm too embarrassed of my panic attacks to admit them to anybody, so I got pretty good at hiding them, even when I was in the middle of one. *That's skill.*

"The shack in the middle of the forest was also raided when we raided the trailer."

Is that the new word for "warrant"?

"This was a much bigger raid than the first home we searched. We also had a warrant to search the shack, and good thing we did. We found two women shackled to the wall in that shack, as well as one in the back bedroom of the trailer. There wasn't anyone there that day when you got inside to take photos, but there certainly was when we arrived."

"Wait a second, there were two girls inside that little shack? I wasn't even that far from them all those days I was up in the deer blind watching that house. I even thought I heard something in the building but passed it off as being an animal or something, and I never went over to look inside." I was beyond shocked and feeling overwhelmed with guilt. I was out there while there were two girls held hostage inside that thing? "Detective Joe, I had no idea they were there." I was near tears when Detective Joe interrupted me and said "Julie, relax ... they are going to be alright and we don't know for sure if they were even there at the same time you were." Detective Joe gave me a stern look but didn't chastise me. I think maybe he was a little proud of me for having the guts to do what I did. Now I really wish I had taken the time to look inside that thing. I was so sure it was just an old run-down shack nobody had used in years.

***

Detective Joe went on to tell me that there were two women in the shack around the age of twenty to twenty-five, and by the time the SWAT team rescued them out of there they were near death. He told me they weren't even sitting on anything other than the hard wood floor, and they were shackled to the wall. They were severely beaten, drugged, dehydrated, and almost starved to death.

"Why in the hell were they in there? And why were they beaten and starved? Are these people serial killers or something?"

"Julie, worse, they are human traffickers, and we have reason to believe that you and possibly your daughter were being targeted by them."

This just got personal.

I had so many questions, and the fact that I was a target of theirs wasn't my first.

"What else did you find?"

Detective Joe told me that it would all become clear soon, but they still had to raid the rest of the homes. Right now, Joe said he was going to take me home to pack, and Stephanie and I were being moved into a safe house that would be heavily guarded. I'm sure I am not too well liked by anyone from any of these homes, and it really was terrifying to learn I was probably targeted. But do we really need to go to these lengths? What about my life? What about work and Stephanie's pre-school? What about my family?

However, maybe Detective Joe knew more than I about these things. If they would kill James, they certainly would have no problem killing me, too. On the way to pick up Stephanie I was a nervous wreck. Detective Joe assured me that they already had police stationed outside of the babysitter's house. *That's impressive.* Joe assured me that I would be in good hands, and safe until all these people were behind bars. I never realized life could change this fast. I used to hear that it can change in the blink of an eye. Well, I guess so. I blinked, and life changed. It happened just that fast, too. We picked Stephanie up, caravanned back to my apartment, and the detectives waited outside while we packed. I was so nervous I could barely think straight, and almost forgot to pack most of our toiletries and things we used every day. Stress can do that to you. I couldn't think straight for a long time after that. One major thing I couldn't do anymore was live my life as I once had.

I had to quit my job again, and just hid out where I could be safe. The police went in and packed up the rest of my apartment and brought everything over to our new secure one. I couldn't tell any of my family where I was, and I certainly couldn't talk to anyone, either. Not anyone in my family, and especially not any of my friends. Unfortunately, my little informant wouldn't be able to find me, either, but once I told the police about my mail box being the drop off for their daily letters, they kept that box available just for them. The police also decided to maintain my apartment for me so we could go back to living there when this was over. That was a relief, I finally liked where we lived. Every other place we'd lived since Stephanie was born was a total dump. I was finally getting on my feet, getting things together, and then this happened.

I thought surveillance was boring, but being in hiding was even worse. We couldn't go anywhere or do anything. The only thing I didn't miss was my job at the hospital. It was really time for me to get out of that place, but I never thought I would end my career there like this. I often wondered what they thought about all of this, or were they even told anything? I asked once what they told my employer, and Detective Joe said he wasn't sure. I didn't buy it, but what did it really matter? My life as I knew it had changed, quite possibly forever. I just worried what this could be doing to Stephanie. She was just a little girl and couldn't understand what was happening. I could barely understand it myself.

The communication through my mailbox continued on a daily basis. I was getting more and more information as the days went by. It was a very interesting read, that's for sure, but it was also starting to seem strange to me, and I started to question if any of it were real. I just couldn't imagine people doing things like this to other people, however, I also saw those shackles in that bedroom, so how could I not believe it? It was almost beyond my ability to comprehend it all.

The person behind those cryptic letters has finally informed me that she's a victim of this group and was once trafficked by them. *Her story was incredible.* She was an insider who lived in these homes and endured their torture. Who better than her to tell her story. It was intense and hard to believe what she was telling me, hard to understand that people could do something like this to others. *It was beyond evil.* Each day she woke up not knowing what she would face that day, or if they would even keep her alive. She told me they kept her drugged most of the time. She said she was used by multiple men for sex every single day that she was there. I can't begin to imagine what it must have been like for her. She told me Christmas Day was the worst day of her life. She lost count of how many men used her that day after she got up to around ninety.

Personally, I would rather be dead. She told me she finally escaped with the help of a few other victims. They were able to secure some big strong men who volunteered to help get some of the other girls out. My question is, why didn't these men go straight to the police and blow this wide open? It doesn't make any sense to me. They risked their own lives to rescue these girls, but they didn't get any backup from the cops? There has to be more to this. I'm sure there's a real reason they avoided getting the police involved and I think I have the answer. Why else would you not go to the police? Maybe they had some knowledge or feared some of the police officers were involved, too. Kind of reminds me of the mafia. They had lots of police officers on the payroll to keep their activities secret.

Could there be some dirty cops on the force?

❧ 12 ❧

The last letter I received from my informant was the most explosive of all. The detectives were now getting my mail for me. At the time, I wasn't aware they were reading the letters before they even gave them to me. Detective Joe delivered this letter to me and told me he didn't know if I should read it or not. *That just made me want to read it all the more.*

"Why, Joe, what in the world could possibly be in that letter that I shouldn't read?"

"Well, Julie, it has information about you in it."

"Well then, I definitely should read it, don't you agree?"

"Ok, Julie, here's the letter, but consider yourself warned. Once you read it you can't un-read it."

"Very funny, Detective Joe."

I opened the letter and silently read what was inside. I was in complete and total shock when I finished reading the words on those pages. This time it wasn't cutouts from a magazine anymore. It was hand written and quite long. The girl who had been my secret informant finally gave me her name, *Emma.*

She claimed to be my sister. *My sister?* This doesn't make any sense, I don't have a sister. She said that I was, in fact, part of this group because we were both born into the group. She said even though I had escaped, they kept their own kind of surveillance on me once they were able to find where I was living. They laid low, and when it came time to get me back, they made their move with James. Even Mary, who I thought was my good friend … she said Mary was involved, too. *This can't possibly be true, how in the hell is Mary involved with any of this?* I helped Mary when we first met at the hospital, and then we became best friends. Mary would never, ever fraud me, and I know she would never lie to me. I don't believe this letter. I was getting angry and about to toss the letter in the garbage when Joe noticed and stopped me.

Then Emma lowered another bomb on me and told me I have another sister, and she is still stuck on the inside, and desperately needs our help.

"Detective Joe, this is total garbage. I don't believe a word of it."

"Julie, I know it's hard to believe, but we have many reasons to believe she might not be lying. *We believe she's telling us the truth.*"

As soon as those words left the detective's mouth my mind flashed back to all the déjà vu I was having at these homes, especially when we were out in the woods. Could this be the reason why? Could Emma really be telling me the truth? I don't know how *or if* I even want to try to wrap my head around any of this now. I mean, at what point is it just too darn much to take? I feel like I am at that point now. No, the truth is, I feel like I'm beyond that point, and I just need to get the hell out of here and away from all of this. I need to go somewhere so I can think and get my head on straight. *But where can I go?*

I know what this is, this is another panic attack. Every time I had a panic attack I wanted to run away and go somewhere safe. *Wherever the hell that might be.* However, what I'm really running from is myself. I can't run from any of this, and I certainly can't go anywhere alone, even if I wanted to. It's not just me I need to worry about, it's Stephanie, too. None of this feels real. I feel like I'm living the worst nightmare ever, and I really wish I could just wake up from it already. However, what if everything Emma said really was true? The new revelations Emma gave us concerning this faction of individuals are extraordinary. If everything in her letters is true, then I really did stir up a hornets' nest. If I am strong enough to handle this I can be instrumental in saving many lives. All from a nobody-girl who worked as an admitting clerk and accepted a date with a monster. Have I really been given a second chance to make this world a better place?

After reading this letter I believe now that this really is bigger than anyone could have ever imagined. Pedophile ring, human trafficking that spanned many other countries. I'm still that girl who few people know and who nobody knows. Most don't know, including even myself, what I was even involved with. There are still too many questions. How was I a part of any of this? They said they wanted to expose these people for the abuse and horrible things they were doing. Abuse and neglect and unlawful treatment of children. It's just too much.

It was horrible reading about the horrific treatment these victims endured. Mostly women, some girls, a few boys, and … children. *Children.* I had never seen any children inside any of the homes. I wonder if there are other homes, I'm not aware of. If it hadn't been for this brave girl, we probably never would have found out what was going on inside these evil homes. I hope we are finally able to bust it wide open and put an end to it. There were also pictures included in those letters that would make even the strongest person cringe. Such a brave anonymous girl who now is telling me she's my sister, Emma. If she really is my sister, then I am proud to know, and I guess I should say be related to such a brave girl. She's the hero that took the chance and risked her life by giving me the knowledge we needed to destroy this evil empire.

Who else but her to tell the story, since she was living inside these homes? She said she explained everything to me as it is now and as it used to be inside these dreadful places. I can't even call them homes because they really aren't homes. They are dens of hell. To me, she's definitely the heroine in this story. Heroes come in many forms. Maybe I can be a heroine in this story, too. However, I'm still scared to death. But then I get this little voice in the back of my head telling me: *Heroes aren't perfect.* Sometimes heroes are scared, but that's just because the thing they're facing is super important, and nobody else is going to go fight it because nobody else has got the guts.

Maybe that one person really is me.

I should have known all those days of sitting in that nasty deer blind that I was strong enough to handle all of this. Hell, I couldn't even tell Detective Joe I was doing that for fear he wouldn't let me. And why wouldn't he let me? Because it was too dangerous. I am strong, I really can do this. If I have a sister still held prisoner inside this godforsaken hell hole, then I need to go find her and rescue her now. I don't think I can tell the detectives about this, especially not Detective Joe. But if I make a mistake this time I really might get myself killed.

Hey, I have an idea. *Far-fetched,* yes, but still an idea. I could go inside these homes as an undercover victim and wear a mic. *Except for the fact that I'm in hiding and they already know what I look like.* I happen to have a friend in the entertainment business. He is so masterful with makeup he can make me look completely different than I do, and with his help I bet they wouldn't even recognize me. I think it is time for me now to communicate back to my sister. I need her help again. I'm going to go talk to Detective Joe first, though. I have to do this the right way. I have to do something, I can't just sit here dying of boredom day after day after day after day ... *after dreadfully boring day.*

These monsters aren't just brainwashing these victims, they are drugging them, too. They really are a bunch of cowards who exploit women and children. They need to be stopped, not just here, but now it seems as if this is a worldwide operation. I really can't fathom it all, but as I said before ... I'm Nancy freaking Drew, and I was put in this position for a reason, so I'm going to go for it. Back to my original question to myself of, "am I strong enough to handle this?" The answer to that question is, "Yes." Who else would be crazy enough to go through with this? My next hurdle will be getting Detective Joe to sign off on it.

"Oh, come on Joe, why not?"

"Well, Julie, for one they already know who you are, and if you step foot inside one of these homes, they will kill you. We don't need you going in there and getting more information. We probably have enough already to put these monsters behind bars."

"But Detective, this isn't just happening here locally, this could be a worldwide operation, and I need to get to the bottom of who's in charge and find out just how far the reach is."

Joe looked almost surprised when I said that, but he still wouldn't budge.

"Julie, we know it would help to get someone in there wearing a wire to get more on them, but I'm not willing to risk you."

"OK, then, would you risk a guy named Bruce?"

"Who is Bruce?"

"I have a friend in the movie business who is willing to come here and turn me into Bruce with lots of makeup and using the different tricks only Hollywood knows."

"Hey, excellent idea, genius, but the answer is still 'no.' Like anyone would believe you're a guy." *There goes his famous eye-roll again.*

"Come on, please, Detective Joe? I didn't want to tell you this, but I think I have another sister still inside. I need to do this myself because I don't think she will trust anyone else."

"OK, if I'm stupid enough to let you do this, what are the odds that you can even find your sister and rescue her?"

"I don't know, but I have to try."

"Julie, forget it, the answer is no. Let me rephrase it, hell no!"

OK, yes, I know Detective Joe ... blah blah blah

I know I'm becoming a big pain in his butt, but I really don't know what else to do. If we are going to prove that this is really what my gut is telling me it is, we will need more proof.

I decided it was time to send my own letter to my now known informant sister, Emma. I need more answers. I want to know if she can tell me which one of these houses my, *our* sister is being held at, and if I try to go undercover as a man, does she think I would be successful? I also wanted to know if the rescue group Emma was involved with would be able to assist me in any way. I don't want to risk Emma's safety since she was already on the outside, but I wonder if any of the men who helped her escape would be willing to go undercover. It was worth asking about.

I wanted to go in armed with as much information as I could possibly get. I wrote her back with all my questions, and left to go tuck the letter inside my old mailbox. It was a risky move, but right now I don't feel I have a choice. I did buy some pepper spray just in case I needed something to protect me. I drove over to my old apartment complex and put the letter inside the mailbox. I didn't have a letter yet from Emma, so that was a good thing she hadn't been there yet. I hope she wasn't finished writing me letters because I desperately wanted her to come back and get mine.

Instead of leaving right away I decided to hang out in my car and watch for a bit. I remember this surveillance thing, oh yeah, I remember this. I change my mind, this is way more boring than hiding out in a safe house. At least I can move around and watch TV or something. This is just sitting and watching. I could never do this as a profession, it would kill me. I sat there for maybe half an hour. I was getting nervous and about to leave when I saw a car pull up in front of the apartments near the mailboxes. *Could this be Emma?* Nope, it's a really big guy getting out of the car. I was relieved to see him walk over to the mailboxes and put something inside one of them. Maybe he's delivering Emma's letters for me. *This is rather interesting.* Maybe Emma isn't my sister at all, maybe she's really my brother. Or perhaps he's just helping her out and being the drop off person. I wouldn't blame her, she's probably playing it safe, just like I am. Maybe he's one of the guards she hired to help her escape. He's a really big guy. I could easily see him as a bodyguard. He certainly wasn't the mailman, either. What the heck's going on?

I have an even better idea. I need to find out who this man is. He would be the perfect choice to go undercover instead of me. I might be willing to go in dressed like a man, but the problem is, no matter how much makeup they use on me, they still can't make me look taller.

I'm very short, and I wouldn't make a very convincing or intimidating guy. Maybe we can use this person instead. He definitely looked intimidating to me.

I have to say, that I, as well as the detectives are surprised that these other homes are still in operation. The police already raided two of them, you'd think that word would have spread to the others by now. There's a total of eleven homes that I'm aware of. I wouldn't be at all surprised if there were more we didn't know about. Could it be possible that they don't know, *that we know*, they are all connected? I bet that's it. Even though I went to these homes and pointed them out to Detective Joe, we weren't able to talk to the people inside all of them. Plus, we were only asking them if they had seen James lately, and to let him know we wanted to talk to him. They might not suspect anything connected with us.

This is really the perfect time to get someone wired up and inside one or more of these homes. This would turn out to be a pretty big break for our investigation. We were finally making some headway on this whole enterprise. I'm shocked still at how brazen or perhaps stupid these people in the rest of these homes are. If it were me and two homes connected to mine were already raided I would have already gotten the hell out of there. All we can conclude is they don't think we know they're connected. *Lucky break for us.*

Emma is such a brave girl. She got information inside one of these homes and quickly got a message back to me, or should I say, *my mailbox*, within a couple days. Before she wrote me back, I had already placed another letter inside the mailbox suggesting we use the same guy who was delivering her letters to my mailbox. I had to come clean with her that I was sitting nearby hoping to get a look at her, and saw him instead. She was cool with it and said she understood why. She said she definitely wanted to meet face to face with me someday, but we'd have to wait until this was all over with. I was so excited to meet my sister, but I still understood the gravity of the job we needed to accomplish.

Emma let me know that the guy who picked up the mail was named

Ray, and he had already offered to go inside wearing a wire for us. That was a big relief. I was getting more and more concerned that I would be taking too big of a risk, or that I wasn't really capable enough to take on that kind of a role. Ray, however, knew some of the people inside these homes, so he's the best choice to put in there without tipping anyone off. I received another new piece of information. Emma gave me more proof that my best friend Mary was involved, and even though I didn't want to believe it, the proof was right in front of my face in this new letter.

Mary, I was told, is a madame who was assigned to take care of the girls in one of their homes. She helps transport them, keeps them drugged, and acts as a sort of mother figure to them. *I'm going to be sick.* Now I can't help but wonder, was anything I had been through with Mary even real? Was she really my friend, or had she just been playing a part like James was? I felt so completely betrayed by her. I don't ever want to talk to her again. But then I realize I have a part to play now, too, so that really wasn't an option. I'm going to have to fake it and not let her in on what's going on. This might be the most difficult job of all.

Emma clued me in on another very important little detail. Even though she's on the outside, she still has people she communicates with on the inside. She told me that her inside informant wanted her to tell me that some people in the group are wondering where I am. Even Emma noticed I'm not at my apartment anymore, and that I'm not showing up at work anymore. Worse was when she let me know that the higher up and more dangerous people in the group were beginning to take notice, too. She said that alone could easily be putting me in more danger. I don't want to do it, but I think I need to go back to living my life exactly as I was living it. I need to talk this over with Detective Joe. I'm scared to death to go back to my life right now without the security of being in a safe house. I'm even more frightened to go back to working at the hospital where I could be an easier target, but if this has a chance of working, that's probably exactly what I need to do. I have come so far, I can't possibly turn back now. I know I have a daughter to think about and she needs her mom, but I am doing this for her, too. I fear if I don't get to the bottom of this her life could end up being the one in danger. I also have a strong belief that as a mother I need to show my daughter how to be strong and how to be a good adult. Mostly, I want to show her how important it is to do the right thing. It's really my daughter that motivates me to keep moving forward. My daughter is the one who gives me most of my strength and determination.

Hopefully, Detective Joe will go along with everything, clear Ray to go undercover and infiltrate these houses as well as get me back to living my life. I could just lie and say I took a little time off work and was staying with some friends to get away or something like that. Maybe I should start trusting Emma more, too. Maybe I shouldn't lie to her at all. I really do need to tell her the truth, because she's been so instrumental in helping me. I have to believe she has my back as well. She really needs my help, too, so I think it is time we started acting like partners. I will be honest and tell her the truth, right after I talk to Detective Joe. I still can't believe the stuff she said about Mary. I trusted Mary with everything. I told her all my deepest secrets and I thought we had a really close friendship. I cared about Mary as if she were a sister. I really helped her get her life back together, too. *Was any of that real?*

Now I'm beginning to wonder if Frank, Mary's boyfriend, was also involved. Is everyone around me involved? Am I surrounded by bad guys? Who can I really trust? The only person I trust right now is Detective Joe, but how do I know he's not involved? I really have to trust someone, so it's got to be Joe. I'm sure he wouldn't have gone to all the trouble he already has if he were any part of this. I'm probably just paranoid. I don't have a reason for being suspicious, especially of Detective Joe. My problem is, my past comes back to haunt me sometimes. I am a very trusting person *too trusting sometimes* and I have had people take advantage of my trust before. And now, with this new information about Mary, it's starting to make me suspicious of everyone. This is something I've really struggled with in the past. If one guy is bad then they're all bad. It's not fair to lump everyone into the same category. I have to remind myself sometimes that not all people are bad. On a positive note, I know that I am fortunate enough to have a very powerful intuition that never steers me wrong. It's when I ignore it I get into trouble. However, I have heard of dirty cops before, but mostly from television. I'm sure there's some amount of truth to everything we hear. Whether it's fact or fiction. I wish this whole situation wasn't real and I could just wake up from this never-ending nightmare. However, my intuition is urging me to believe there could be some dirty cops involved with this.

Convincing Detective Joe was a lot easier than I had imagined. I think it's probably because my new idea was to put a guy in there instead of me. I really didn't think he would ever agree to letting me do it, anyway. Sometimes I need to consider my own safety, too, though. It probably would have been reckless and stupid for me to even try it. I don't know who these people are, but if I've learned anything by now, it should be that these are very dangerous people.

I'm aware of the risks but I'm doing this for those innocent people trapped inside these homes. I'm also doing this for my daughter. I don't want garbage like this around when she's older. Sad to think that this kind of thing probably will still be around, unfortunately. I really hope through my own efforts to educate her she will keep herself safe from this kind of scum. I will do everything I can to raise her right and keep her safe from these and all monsters.

I'm remembering a situation a long time ago when I was almost a human trafficking victim, myself. Now I wonder how close I came.

Years ago, when I worked at a bank, I waited on a customer who owned a local magic shop. It was a husband who ran the shop and his wife usually came into the bank to make their bank deposits. This was many years ago when I wasn't even twenty yet. Long before Stephanie was even a thought.

One day, the wife came into the bank to make a deposit and I happened to wait on her. It was a busy Friday afternoon, so I didn't have much time to chat, people were lining up behind her, so I was trying to hurry through her deposits. She leaned over the counter a little and quietly asked me if I would be interested in working a second job. I asked her what kind of a job. *I was always looking to make more money.*

She said it was for their new business called, "The French Quarter." I instantly thought she was opening a new restaurant. We already had a local restaurant called "The Hindquarter" so I thought they were playing off of its popularity. So when I asked her what my duties would be, she said she would need to speak to me in private about that. I was surprised with her answer because although I only had experience as a hostess, I liked the idea of becoming a waitress so I could make tips.

So, I said to her, "Well, the only thing I would be qualified to do right away is hostess, but I would love to eventually get trained as a waitress."

"You must have misunderstood, we are a massage parlor."

I was blown away, and without realizing it I blurted out, "Oh, hell no." I felt really bad about having that kind of a reaction until years later, when I read in our local newspaper they were busted for drugs and prostitution. I wonder if they were human trafficking girls there, too, and she just wanted to use me for things I am better off not knowing about.

She definitely had her eyes on me for a long time after that. Every time she came into the bank she made some comment to me about working for her. Now that I know what they were really doing, I believe she just wanted to use me. I was really angry, yet terrified, at how close I had come to being involved. It just goes to show you really don't know who some people are. It's a scary world out there and I have started to realize just how much and how sheltered I must have been from it all. I was really in the dark. I didn't know that the "French Quarter" was really a place somewhere in France that was mainly there for prostitution.

I really must be pretty naïve.

My senior award in high school was "Most Naïve," and I guess I was still doing a really great job living up to the title. It was pretty funny when I got the award, though. We had to go up on a stage in front of the whole student body to accept our individual awards. When they called my name, the school erupted in laughter. I didn't know what to say when I had to accept it, so I said the only thing that came to my mind. "Thanks, everyone, for my senior award, even though I don't know what the word naïve means."

I heard a guy in the audience yell out, "That's why you got the award."

Hey, any kind of attention was good attention in my book back in those days. I had a horrible mother, so these fine people I went to school with really provided me with the "love supply" I so terribly needed. I wasn't upset about the award, and of course I knew what the word "naïve" meant. I really did deserve it, too, I must admit. You could tell me pretty much anything back then and I would believe it.

I really don't want to be naïve anymore.

❧ 13 ❧

Detective Joe, much to my surprise, was very open to sending this new "Ray" guy inside. Joe also agreed that we needed more evidence to go on to put an end to this operation, once and for all. Ray came into the station a couple days later and the police did their vetting thing to approve him for his mission. They wired him up, gave him instructions on what to do, who to get information from, etc., and sent him on his way.

I was really nervous for Ray. I was praying every day that he would be safe and able to get us the information we needed. Hopefully nobody got suspicious because this boy was really wired up. They had listening devices attached to him, and secret cameras inserted into his hat as well as the sides of his new glasses. Such an array of really cool spy equipment they've come up with to help gather information without getting caught, it's pretty impressive.

As for me, I talked, or should I say conned, Detective Joe into letting me move back into my life again. Detective Joe told me he would position some police to keep an eye on me but wouldn't tell me where they were or who they were. He wanted it to look as normal as possible while still keeping me safe. That idea I really liked because I was nervous going back to my life unprotected. Even though I tried to figure out who and where the police were, I never did. That actually gave me more peace of mind. If even I can't spot them, then there's a good chance that nobody else will either. The police got me my job back at the hospital after talking to the head person there about our secret mission. I sure hope they are able to keep my secret and not let on to what I'm doing. I fear I'm in enough danger as it is. My first night back was really scary, and I never stopped looking over my shoulder, but as time went on it became easier. My old routine was back and I was glad.

Even Mary didn't act any differently toward me, but I had a tough time acting the same towards her. Luckily, I managed to be the same person enough to keep her from getting suspicious. I had no choice but to keep up the pretense with Mary. One strange thing about Mary, though, she stopped asking me if I wanted to hang out with her. I guess her duties at the human trafficking house were too demanding. She and Frank were fake living together, too. I didn't see Frank for a really long time, and then one day she invited me to come over for dinner and play some board games. I couldn't *not* go because it would look suspicious. I knew I had to go and do my best to act normal. The weirdest people were there, people I had never met before, and people Mary had never, ever talked to me about. She just waved her hand when I asked her about them and said they were mostly people Frank knew, and that was that.

When we started playing board games I was flabbergasted when Mary poured herself a glass of wine, and then she asked me if I would like one.

"Mary, what the hell are you doing? You know you shouldn't drink."

Mary just dismissed me again and told me she's able to drink responsibly now, and it's not a problem for her anymore. I didn't buy it because I know what Mary is like when she drinks. I still have the scar to prove it. I wanted to run out of the house at that very instant but realized I had to play it cool. I stayed for a few games and then made some tired excuse to leave. Mary got shitfaced and was acting like a lunatic. *Big shocker.* She slipped and started referring to some people as "her girls."

"Mary, who are you talking about when you say, 'your girls?'"

Frank got worried and pitched in with, "Oh, Julie, you know how Mary gets when she drinks."

"Hey, Frank, can you and I go talk for a moment, *in private?*"

"How about we talk later? Tonight isn't a good time, and I don't want to upset Mary."

And with that, I was out of there.

That really sucked. My best friend Mary was a complete, total fraud. I have been hurt many times in my life by past relationships but this time, learning that who I thought Mary was, and finding out who she really is, was tough. Mary had become like family to me. I didn't have many friends, my family really wanted nothing to do with me, either, so this was difficult.

As far as my mother goes, she really never wanted anything to do with me. She was narcissistic and abusive and acted like she was in some weird kind of competition between me and my father. The closer I got to my father, the more she hated me. Well, not my real father, my real father mysteriously died when I was little. This was my stepfather, but to me he was my real father. He always treated me like I was one of his own. He was a very good man and I miss him terribly. He died from a lung disease, and I would give anything to still have him here with me. My mother eventually became so abusive to me I had to finally cut her out of my life. I never felt love from my mother and I always wondered why she even had me.

For someone like me to lose a friend, that's a hard thing to deal with. Mary isn't and never was my friend, and that reality hit me like a brick. I cried all the way home that night, mourning a friend that never was. How do you mourn a friend that never was a friend? That's a new one for me. I mourned her like I had lost a sister, because I had come to think of Mary as my sister. I went from mourning her to being really, really angry at her, and that could end up being dangerous for me.

There really is a fine line between love and hate…

***

It had only been one week since Ray went undercover, but the detectives think they finally have enough information to raid the rest of the homes.

Ray has been doing a remarkable job of filming things nobody would ever want to see and listening in on incriminating conversations nobody would ever want to hear. He was the perfect person to send in there, instead of me. I probably would've been spotted the first hour because my fear would have taken over and gave me away. I'm a big chicken, but Ray was very brave and very determined to break this cult apart.

There was a total of sixteen houses involved, and I was only aware of eleven. That was really shocking to learn. Ray had been pulled out, and now not only are the police and the SWAT team involved, they have called in the National Guard as well to orchestrate raiding all these properties at the same time. I am blown away this is happening so fast. They're about to raid all of these homes, at the same time.

These guys are the real heroes.

The following day I was driving through downtown after work when I noticed a ton of activity at a local bank. Actually, it just so happened to be the bank that I used to work at, the same bank where the lady tried to lure me into prostitution. The bank is swarming with police, and as I drive by I even see police dogs so excited they are about to tear free from their handlers. What could possibly be happening? I decided to pull over and park for a moment so I could watch. They were taking boxes and boxes of documents out of the bank. This looks so weird to me. Why in the world is there a raid on my old bank? Then I see, off in the distance, my old friend Detective Joe, and I knew this had to have something to do with the raid on the homes.

The raid on the homes hadn't happened yet, so it's a mystery why they were raiding the bank. Not only are the police there, I also see some men wearing jackets with the word "FBI" on the back. This is just so freaking weird. So weird that the bank I used to work at is now being raided. What in the world is this new connection? Whatever this was, it looked pretty intense to me.

I decided not to bother Detective Joe right now. If he wanted me to know what was going on, he certainly would have told me. I didn't want to get in the way. I drove away and went to pick Stephanie up from the babysitters. Luckily the babysitter I had was also an undercover police officer, so I didn't have to worry too much about Stephanie's safety when I was away. If there was any time in my life when I needed some peace of mind, now was the time. I waited and waited all night, hoping that Detective Joe would return my call, but I never heard from him. I wasn't that surprised, I'm sure he was extremely busy with what just went down at the bank. My curiosity about that situation almost kept me awake all night. It's so hard to sleep these days. Every time I try I have so many thoughts popping up inside my head that I can't possibly relax enough to sleep. It's incredibly annoying. Aside from James tricking me and now Mary, could this bank job have been their first attempt to get me into this human trafficking ring? If it even is truly a human trafficking ring, I still don't know that for sure. If I can believe what I'm being told it is. The lady who tried to hire me as a massage therapist, was she the very first attempt? *And why me?*

I finally heard back from Detective Joe. He wouldn't tell me anything on the phone, but asked me if I could come down to the station, he would fill me in there. We were still worried I was being watched, and we were pretty certain my home phone was tapped again. What a horrible feeling of violation. It's the same feeling you'd get when your home just was robbed and the robber went through your underwear drawer. It's creepy as hell to know someone was watching you and listening in on your conversations. I was able to drive right away to the police station, almost too excited yet nervous because I was anxious to hear what Detective Joe was going to tell me.

"Detective Joe, did you get my message to call me back? I was driving down the middle of downtown yesterday when I saw the swarm of police, FBI, and excited police dogs, and it appeared as if you had just raided the bank. The bank I used to work at, no less."

"Yes, that's exactly what we were doing. The bank manager has been arrested for being involved with the human trafficking ring we are about to bust wide open, as well as funding their entire operation and laundering money for them." *That's all?*
I was shocked to hear what Detective Joe just shared with me, but by no means was I prepared for what was about to come.

"Julie, I don't know how to tell you this, but we need to put you and Stephanie back into hiding until the raid *we are planning for tomorrow* is over. There's so much I need to tell you that will be excruciatingly difficult for you to hear.

Unfortunately, I can't tell you anything until this operation is over. I can tell you that you have been hugely instrumental in helping us bring down one of the largest human trafficking rings in North America. It's not just happening here in our country, it's a global operation. Many countries across the globe are involved, and they will eventually be brought down, too. I shouldn't be telling you this right now but I'm going to anyway. I'm so proud of your bravery and how willing you were to help us. Yes, you took some risks we would never have approved of, but it's really what broke this thing wide open. Without you, we may never have been able to do what we are about to do. When this is all over you are going to be rewarded with a very special medal from the President himself representing a grateful nation. That's about all I can tell you."

That's all.

Now I know this isn't real. I'm just a regular girl, I'm nobody special. I'm getting some kind of medal from the President? I must be dreaming again. *This is crazy.* What kind of medal could it possibly be? *Medal for bravery, maybe?* Did Nancy Drew ever get awarded a medal? The hard part is waiting. I'm very excited to know that I did something good and positive in the world and perhaps I was even able to help save some of the girls inside these homes. Hopefully many others, too.

I really wish I could talk to Ray. I need to know for sure if in fact I really do have another sister still stuck inside. I guess I will find everything out by the end of the week. More and more things keep piling on top of already huge piles of weirdness. How in the world am I supposed to relax now? Here we go again, back to the safe house. Well, at least I know that we will be as safe as possible while these homes get raided tomorrow. I bet they are planning on doing the raid in the early morning hours when everyone is most likely still asleep. I've seen it done that way on television before. I know that everything we have uncovered so far is connected, even as far back as my first job at the bank, combined with my déjà vu experiences everywhere I went with the detective, plus my intuition constantly warning me.

Stephanie and I spent a very sleepless night at the safe house, surrounded this time by police, FBI agents, and undercover security guards that dressed like the president's secret service security. *The men in black.* There were even police as well as other security guards perched on the roof of the house with guns. I think they were probably trained snipers. This was incredibly scary and intense, but at the same time, super exciting.

I have a strange feeling again that what I'm about to find out could be a life changer for me. I don't know why, but it almost feels like someone or something is trying to prepare me for the worst. Someone on a spiritual level perhaps is trying to prepare for what I'm about to hear, what could potentially change everything I know about myself and change everything I thought was real. I feel as if I'm on the brink of discovering everything I believed about my life was all just one big lie.

Be careful of what you wish for.

❧ 14 ❧

It felt like it took forever for Detective Joe to come back to the safe house. I was getting pretty nervous, and worried about everyone's safety. I wasn't at all prepared for what I was about to hear. *Nobody could have prepared me for any of this.* It felt like a dream, I felt almost like I was floating, as if I were having another out-of-body experience.

I've heard people referring to this as disassociation before, and now I can definitely relate to how it feels. It was more a feeling of wanting to dis-associate from my own feelings, thoughts and in my case, what had been going on in my life. At least this time I didn't have to leave my body. It was excruciatingly painful to re-enter. I hope I never have to go through anything like it again.

After about a week Detective Joe finally called. He said they were still very busy gathering information. He told me they had been very successful with the raid and had arrested everyone associated with all sixteen of the houses. They were busy interrogating them and were almost done. He said he would be coming by to see me within the next couple days. He told me he had some very important information to share with me, and he thought it would answer most of my questions. He wanted to warn me that some of the things he had to tell me would be difficult for me to hear, but he felt he had an obligation to tell me everything.

Now I really feel apprehensive. What in the world is he going to tell me? I had a feeling it would probably change my life forever. How does he expect me to wait a couple days? I had no idea what I was about to learn. This entire investigation had only been going on for a couple months, but it felt a lot longer. I have to wonder, will my life ever be the same again?

What was Detective Joe trying to prepare me for?

Detective Joe was sitting at the kitchen table the following morning when I woke up. I was surprised to see him, I wasn't expecting him to come talk to me so soon. *I was excited and scared all at the same time.*

"Good morning, sunshine, I brought a friend along with me. This is Maria. She works in our department as a grief counselor."

Grief counselor? Why do I need a grief counselor?

"Nice to meet you, I am only here to help wherever I can and only if you want me to. It's entirely up to you." *Maria was very kind and instantly put me at ease.*

"Detective Joe, with all due respect to Maria, why do you think I need a grief counselor?"

"Honestly, Julie, I don't think you need a grief counselor per se, however, Maria is more than a grief counselor. Maria has proven herself to be a darn good counselor in many areas, and I thought you would feel comfortable with her. She's also had lots of experience counseling girls that were involved in the sex trade. I wanted her here to help assist me today because of the sensitive nature of the information I came to share with you."

Sensitive nature?

Spill it, Detective Joe...

"Julie, some of this is going to be very tough for you to hear. Some of it I think you are already sensing with some of the déjà vu stuff you've had going on. By the way, how in the world were you able to sense all that stuff?"

"I already told you, I'm psychic."

Detective Joe doesn't believe in all that stuff. Of course, he doesn't. First, he's a guy, and guys are known for being skeptics, plus he's a detective, which just adds another layer of "show me some proof" on top of it all. Most of the conversation became a blur, but the main most important message was clear. It turns out I was right.

I never mentioned to Detective Joe that my father wasn't really my biological father. I call him my father because he raised me as his own, but I was actually fathered by another man. The man who biologically fathered died from cancer when I was very young, I don't remember him.

"Julie, your biological father was a member of this cult, this human trafficking ring we just busted."

"Shut the hell up Joe, are you kidding me?" *How the heck can I possibly believe this?* Now I see why the counselor was here. I was told when I was very young that my father had died from cancer. Nobody told me anything about any of this. I don't remember my real father at all, in my eyes my adopted father was my real father. Here is the truth about my past, slapping me in my face.

"Julie, I am so sorry to have to tell you that your mother has lied to you about everything. She didn't want you to know any of this, and I went against her wishes by telling you."

"You actually spoke to my mother?"

I hadn't spoken to my mother in over four years. I had to finally accept the fact that my mother just didn't have the ability to love me. It was a tough life growing up with her as a mother. She was abusive, narcissistic, and completely dismissive towards me. That is, when she wasn't telling me how I was going to find her dead when I got home from school. She used a lot of mental torment on me, too. She was both physically and mentally abusive, but the mental stuff stayed with me the longest.

It's a really long and sad story, but to have any kind of life and to heal myself, I had to let her go and go make a life for me and my daughter free of any of her abuse. I am proud to say I was successful in ending the cycle of abuse for my daughter. Of course, she thinks she was the most perfect mother, and is the first to tell anyone who will listen what a great mother she is. She's a nasty, horrible person who never should've had any children. Now I find out she was involved in this evil human sex trafficking ring. My biological father, too. In a weird way I'm relieved my biological father died so my real father could save me from all of this. *Anyone can be a sperm donor, it takes a real man to be a father.* I can't imagine where I might have ended up. I don't believe my mother would have protected me from anything or anyone in this group. My mother never once had my back or my best interest at heart. I can't imagine treating my own daughter this way, it's so far from who I am and I am thankful for that. But as far as I go, learning this new information about my own mother was not at all surprising to me, not even a little bit.

I will have to deal with my mother later, now I just need to try to digest all the craziness put in front of me. Maybe it's a good thing my mom tortured me my entire life. Maybe it made me a much stronger person, strong enough to handle this. I found out my mother was deeply involved in this group and my biological father worked for them. Basically, my father was what they called a soldier and did as he was ordered. He kidnapped for them, pimped out girls for them, and did various other things I didn't want to know about ... for them.

He had a similar job as James. My biological father was a monster. He was killed in a raid. My mother escaped during the raid and took me with her. I guess she left her other kids behind. I wonder why she only took me. I was told she went to get some help in a shelter, and that's where she met my real father. I won't even claim this first guy *bio guy* as my father. I don't want to come from people like this. It's scary to even think about it. Will I eventually turn into a monster, too? I won't let that happen. My daughter needs me to be strong for her and teach her how to be a good person.

One thing I will say about my mother. Through all of her torture she taught me how to survive, and what kind of mother I wanted to be. I'm grateful for that, at least. I'm grateful for her teaching me I didn't want to be anything close to who she is, and proud of the fact that I succeeded. I am nothing like my mother. However, because I was her daughter, people who hated her also hated me. I guess you could call it guilt by association. I have had on occasion a few different women apologize to me for assuming I was just like my mother. Once they got to know me, they realized I'm the polar opposite of my mother.

The part that bothers me the most is that nobody thought it was important to share any of this information with me. As far as my father goes, he's been dead now for eight years. Not my bio dad, my real dad, the one who was there for me day after day. His name was George. My aunt said he died because he wanted to, to get away from my mother. It sounds kind of preposterous on the surface, but if you knew my mother you wouldn't find it too far-fetched. Personally, I believe she nagged him to death. Either way, she killed him. I wish I could have had the chance to ask him why he never told me about any of this. I get why my mother didn't care to tell me, but why not him? He had to have known the whole sordid story. He should've wanted me to know just in case something like, *what is happening to me now*, ever happened to me. Maybe I could have been more equipped to protect myself.

But then, how could that really have helped? Maybe because I was very young when my mother escaped the cult, he thought I would always be safe from it. I don't know if they used me for sales, and I don't think I want to know. *Disgusting.*

George was a strict Catholic. Unfortunately for me, very strict Catholic. He sent me to Catholic grade school where I was also abused on a daily basis. I had abuse at home and at school. I referred to my childhood as an experiment in terror. It really isn't that surprising I was never told, now that I think about it. The good old Catholic way of sweeping everything under the carpet.

Of course, nobody intended to ever bring up any of my past to me. I had repressed my young memory so deep in the recesses of my mind. If all of this stuff with James hadn't happened, I probably would have never remembered any of it. My childhood was so riddled with crap I hardly remember any of it as it is. Detective Joe told me my mother didn't even seem the least bit ashamed or like she cared when he confronted her. She probably denied everything like she always does. I don't care, she's not a part of my life anymore and I intend to keep it that way.

She needs to stay the hell away from me.

***

What I didn't know is that because I was once considered a member of this human trafficking ring, the wolves were circling around me, coming for me, coming to reclaim me, the human property they still felt they owned, so to speak. Not just me, but my family as well. They came extremely close to succeeding, too. James was just a soldier working for them. *Just a pawn.* He really didn't have any kind of romantic interest in me at all. He was just doing a job.

I know now why he kept pursuing me to date him. It all seemed so strange to me at the time. Any normal guy would have given up after the amount of times I turned him down, but not James. Now I know he was just following orders. My intuition was trying to save me. Perhaps, in the end, it *did* save me.

What's really hard to imagine is my mother being involved with all of this. She always acted so "high society," and wanted everyone to look at her like she was. We had money, but we weren't what I would consider wealthy. My father worked his ass off trying to give her everything she wanted, or should I say, everything she demanded. She was relentless with her demands, too. She could make his life pure hell until he forked over the money for her latest piece of jewelry, new designer clothing item, or her brand-new remodeled home she had to have to keep up pretenses.

I remember she hired a high-end designer that put pink and orange shag carpet in our house. I had to rake it with a rake like you rake leaves outside with. It was hideous and really ugly. She even had to have the latest accessories, and of course, don't get me started on the expensive cars she had to have. I really believe now my father was somehow involved with the mafia. He worked as a manager in a men's clothing store. He worked from morning until night. There were days where I never even saw him because he left for work before I woke up, and got home after I went to bed. I wouldn't think the income of a manager of a small men's clothing store could afford the luxuries he was required to shower on my mother.

However, he went to a lot of clothing shows and came home with the most incredible and interesting stories about the mafia. The mafia was very involved with men's clothing back in the day. I would imagine my father got some kind of "kickback" from working with them. After one of my father's buying trips, he came home and shared a creepy story with us. The man in the room next door to his was found dead with his penis cut off and placed in his own mouth. My father told us that was known as "the calling card" of the mafia. If you ever double-crossed them, this is how they paid you back.

I always had a weird kind of respect and fear for the mafia after hearing that story. I was also very intrigued by them as well. I had a great deal of admiration and respect for my father. My mother was strangely jealous of our relationship, on top of just being absolutely nuts. She was scary crazy, so I tried to stay away from her as much as possible. Perhaps this new information about her involvement, whether it was voluntary or not, might give me a little more insight into why my mother is such a train wreck. I guess it really doesn't matter at this point in time, I still can't have a relationship with her.

Detective Joe was about to share some information with me that was going to help me understand why they brought the grief counselor with them.

"Julie, we have reason to believe your real father sold you when you were very young."

Sold me?

"Exactly what do you mean, Joe, sold me how?"

"Well, Julie, they also refer to it as renting out a young girl to creeps who are attracted to young girls. They also gave birth to children within the group merely for the intention to sell them into human trafficking, or worse."

I don't want to know what the "or worse" part means. I have heard some horror stories, but was that going to be my future? Was I born only for the intention to just be sold? How can I possibly wrap my head around any of this? *This is insane.*

I must have only been around four or five years old. How the hell can anyone look at a child that young and have any kind of sexual thoughts towards them? Then I remembered James. His victim was only four.

I was starting to have anxiety and I think Maria could sense it.

"Julie, do you need a break?"

"No, that's ok, thanks Maria, I'm just having a hard time trying to understand any of this."

Maria patted the back of my hand with hers and said, "I know, dear, I know."

Maria was such a kind and gentle lady. I see why she was so good at helping people. Once I got over the shock of my own father selling me out to creepy old men, I began to cry. I didn't even know my biological father, but just the thought that my own father didn't love me enough to protect me ... it absolutely broke my heart. It was a devastating feeling. I really did need a break, this was just too much to take. I have so much to think about. First of all, I was right about everything I was feeling. I also sensed they had much more to share with me besides this. I'm not much of a drinker, but I really felt like I needed something, something strong, like a top shelf Long Island in the biggest glass I can find.

Anyone up for a drink?

"You know what, Jules, we don't normally go out to bars to deliver information from a raid, but this also isn't anything close to normal. There's a small bar down the street and they rarely are busy, so let's get out of here and go get you a drink. I have a feeling you're going to need one."

I got my top shelf Long Island and the conversation continued. Detective Joe educated me on many aspects of these groups that I was completely unaware of. It was shocking to hear but not surprising. I don't think these people, *monsters, really*, would stop at anything to make a buck. I have known many different monsters growing up, but these monsters take the cake.

I used to think the worst monsters were the religious monsters. For example, priests who molest children and nuns who abuse them. They are wolves hiding behind collars and habits. *This is the uniform of the priests and the nuns.* I always thought they were the worst kind of monsters. People who hide behind God for the sole reason to get access to innocent children so they can abuse them are the worst of the worst. The nuns especially scared the crap out of me. When I was in first grade they thought I was evil because I was left handed. They tied my left hand down to the side of my chair every day trying to break me. I am proud to say that they never succeeded, I am still very much left handed. *What a bunch of stupid, ignorant bitches.* They were just a group of angry, frustrated women who just wanted to take all of their anger and frustrations out on innocent children. However, this human trafficking stuff is a whole other breed of monster. The world desperately needs to be way more educated about these monsters so we can all join together to protect the innocent children from them.

Let me tell you a little about this new breed of monster. They are just out to make a buck off the souls of children and lost women and even some men, too. Mostly women, though. I was right when I thought this could be bigger than anything I could have ever imagined. *It is.* We all know about the illegal escort services, and even though these people are part of that, too, it goes way deeper. They are having babies born only for sex, and this really blew my mind ... satanic rituals. These children are born with the intent to be abused, raped, and tortured. Some are even killed during satanic rituals.

They wanted my baby, not to love, but to use and abuse. They never loved me. My parents never intended to love me. I wasn't born to be their daughter, I was a commodity. The kids were for trafficking only, and they were children for sale. These poor kids would be raped nightly by not just one, but by groups of men. I know this is hard to read, and trust me, it was harder to learn that I was only born to be used, born to be a slave. People are made to be sex slaves for money, and the only ones getting rich are the pimps, the monsters who own these girls. *They are literally owned.* I heard they are actually traded and purchased. What a black mark on humanity this is. Is this worse than how the slaves were treated in the 1800s? I don't know, perhaps. It's not just trafficking for sex, there's also forced labor trafficking, domestic servitude trafficking, and in my opinion the scariest one yet, satanic ritual trafficking.

The detectives also found numerous images of women being tortured or even possibly killed inside these evil homes. They found drugs and various drug and sex paraphernalia. Anything you can imagine that's disgusting, it was inside these homes. I guess the chains and cuffs coming off the bed and the wall wasn't the worst of it. The deeper they looked, the more they found. They found additional evidence that they were selling drugs and laundering money. They even had dirty cops on their payroll so they could cover up for them.

Luckily, these "dirty cops" weren't aware of the detectives' undercover operation. I can't imagine how much more danger that would have put us all in. If they don't put them away forever, I will have to hide again. It's sad, but because of this I will have to keep checking to see if any of them get out. Worse yet, could they be working with some members still free on the outside? That thought terrifies me. Will I ever be completely safe? Will I always have to look over my shoulder?

Detective Joe told me, "Truth is, there are more slaves around the world today than ever before in history."

I'm going to need a moment...

I don't know how to handle any of this information, however, I didn't want Detective Joe to stop telling me everything they found out. It seems like Ray was very instrumental in finding out lots of valuable information while he was undercover. He was able to tape hours of incriminating information, stuff that Detective Joe said should keep these clowns behind bars for the rest of their natural lives. *Oh Lord I hope so.* I shudder to think of what might happen to me if any of them got out and came looking for me ... *again.*

"Hey Detective Joe, were you able to find out anything about the family up in Washington State? I think the father's name was Mike. You know, the ones who were desperately trying to get me to just hand over my baby to them? Supposedly they already had four kids of their own. The ones I lied to about having a miscarriage? What's the story with them, or are they not at all connected to this?"

Detective Joe looked down for a moment, swirling the melting ice in his drink before he began to speak, and I knew something huge was about to be dumped in my lap. I was afraid to know, but desperate to learn the connection and the truth about these weirdos. They really worked me over and tried to make me feel guilty. These people were the worst.

"There's still so much to tell you, Julie, so we might as well start with these people, because they were actually the ringleaders of the group."

What the hell? I knew it! I knew they were after my child for a reason. Sick bastards.

"Julie, they were the ones who instigated this whole thing with you. They were the ones who sent James into the hospital to get you to go out with him and try to get you back into the business."

That Washington contingent, I knew they were just pure evil.

I had to ask Detective Joe what happened to them, and more importantly, what happened to their kids.

"They really didn't have any kids. Or, we weren't able to find any children living in the home when we busted them."

I love it!

"So, they are behind bars, too?"

"Yes, they are, along with a whole lot of others from the regional bust."

The judicial department is going to have to build a bigger jail to house all these freaks. I couldn't believe the Washington family, or what I thought was a family, were the leaders of this whole group of sickos.

"What about the Stepford Wives I met at the New Year's Day house? Whatever happened to them?"

Detective Joe shared with me a rather interesting new problem they were having. There's a strange phenomenon called "Stockholm Syndrome." This is also referred to as a "trauma bond." Sometimes victims develop an emotional attachment to their abusers. This is usually a result of intense stress, total dependence and feeling the need to cooperate just to survive. After a while, the victim begins to defend his or her abuser.

"Their abuser has them so brainwashed into believing they can't survive without them that they begin to legitimately care for their abusers. The police are trying to get them the psychological help they need so they can testify in court against these human traffickers."

The women that were held prisoner inside these homes are now in a safe house themselves. Thank God for that. However, it seems at this time they don't want to testify against their abusers. What could have possibly happened in their minds to cause this bond? Perhaps they have just been drugged for so long they feel they need their abusers so they can keep providing them with their next fix.

What a mess.

All the evidence that Ray was able to provide will probably be enough to put these idiots behind bars for a very long time, *hopefully for the rest of their lives.* They might not even need the testimony of the victims, but it sure would be helpful to know what they know. I would love to talk to some of them, but I don't want to do anything to jeopardize the investigation. I'm having a really tough time trying to come to terms with how I came into this world. Maria was very helpful, and spent most of the day counseling me.

"Maria, it's one thing to learn that your mother has mental issues. It's so much harder to have to accept the fact that she just didn't have the mental capacity to love me. I tried so hard to make her love me that I even tried to buy her love."

"Julie, that's so sad. Why don't we talk a little more about that … can you give me an example of what you did to try to buy her love?"

I went back in my mind to all the times I tried to earn her love. I wondered how many examples Maria wanted because I had many. I will just give her the highlights.

"One time I spent my entire "State Fair" allowance on a turquoise ring I thought she would like. I look back on it now and realize, I was just trying to buy her affection in much the same way I always saw my father do. She gave me the ring back the second I gave it to her. I didn't understand why at the time and it really broke my heart. Now I understand it was just a cheap fair ring and it wasn't good enough for her."

Maria was trying hard not to show any emotion, but I sensed my story was getting to her a little. It wouldn't be the first time I made a counselor cry.

"Julie, would you like to share any other stories about your mother?"

"Alright, here's a good one. Since she didn't love me, or probably didn't even like me, she wasn't too worried about sparing my feelings.

Another time, I climbed up a hill because I found some beautiful blue flowers at the top. I wanted to pick some for her and surprise her with them. I picked a big bouquet of flowers. I was so excited as I rode my bike home with my new gift for her. Surely, she would love these beautiful flowers and in turn, start to love me, too."

"I handed them to her with a big smile on my face, and what does she do? She tells me they are called 'Bachelor Buttons' and they aren't flowers at all, they are weeds. She threw them back at me and told me to throw them away. I walked over to the garbage can with tears streaming down my face. I pretty much knew at that moment my mother was never going to love me, she never intended to have any kind of a loving relationship with me, and I was right."

"That's sad Julie. I'm sorry you had to endure that kind of rejection."

"Maria, I'm feeling a bit like I'm in shock right now. I just don't how I'm supposed to cope with the fact that my biological parents only had me to sell me. It's now been confirmed to me they really had no love for me at all. *That hurts the most.* They would have even sold me to satanic worshipers to be used in a satanic ritual. It's my new reality ... the sick and disturbing was I was brought into this world."

"Julie, you have only begun to work through this. I will be here for you whenever you feel the need to talk. You aren't alone. I've had a lot of experience dealing with situations like this. Trust me, I will get you through this."

The only kind of relationship I have ever had with my mother was one of frustration and anger because she never said a kind word about me, she ruined my self-esteem, and guilted me into doing anything she wanted. I finally had to say enough is enough, but not until I was an adult, and not until a whole lot of mental damage was done to me. But, to now know that my own mother only gave birth to me to sell me. That was a whole new can of worms to deal with.

This new revelation explains a lot to me. My mother is, in fact, a monster.

ᘒ **15** ᘓ

It was way beyond time for us to leave the bar. We were only there for a couple of hours but the conversation was so intense it seemed much longer. We knew better than to have more drinks and we were all glad we decided to walk to the bar instead of drive. We walked down the sidewalk in much needed silence. There's a peace in silence, sometimes. It felt very calming to stroll down the street and watch the lush tree limbs above us blowing in the wind. Some were even dancing shadows on the street as their leaves began to fall. The stories and events of the last few days were flooding my mind. It was incredible and almost overwhelming for me to have my deepest fears and intuition brought to light all in one short afternoon. It was a necessary quiet time and peaceful walk to end this day. I wonder if it felt the same for Joe and Maria. Another question came to mind as we started to walk back inside the house.

"Detective Joe! I can't believe I forgot to ask you this. Do I really have a sister? Was the informant really my sister, and did I have another sister still trapped inside that we needed to rescue?"

"No, Julie, I'm sorry to have to tell you this, but they just call each other sisters. It wasn't meant in a literal way, they all referred to each other as sisters. They referred to their captors as Daddy."

That's really disturbing. They didn't call their captors daddy because they wanted to, they were forced to. *Thanks for sharing, Detective Joe.* I can't begin to imagine the level of mind control, brain washing and other disgusting tactics they used against these poor, innocent girls. Not to mention they are probably all seriously addicted to hard core drugs. I was told they successfully placed all the victims into drug rehabilitation facilities. I thought that was a great thing, but I was surprised by the level of addiction. This must be their main tactic to keep them under control, just keep them drugged all the time. Totally explains all the women at the New Year's Day home that day. I thought they acted weird, and now I know why.

I suspected they were acting like a bunch of drugged zombies, and sadly, they were. I didn't want these innocents to go through any painful withdrawals, and hopefully this can be the beginning of a whole new life for them. They really deserve all the help we can give them. The biggest hurdle, *I fear,* will be getting them to accept the help and not go back to the same life. I'm going to do everything in my power to save each and every one of these girls. I would never give up on any one of them, sisters or not. I was a little sad learning that Emma wasn't really my sister. However, I have never been that close to anyone in my family. My friends were more like family to me. Hopefully Emma and I can continue to build a long friendship together after this is over. My friends are very important to me. These are the people who choose to love me ... not because they are related to me but because they genuinely care about me. You can't pick your family but thank goodness you can pick your friends.

"Hey Joe, I thought I was done, but I guess I still have more questions. What about James, do you know who killed him, and why? Also, what about the surveillance cameras and all the semitrucks that I saw coming and going during my little surveillance of that trailer?"

"OK, so to answer your first question about James, the owner of the trailer killed him. James didn't run because of his legal issues, he ran because he was afraid he was now a target. We still haven't found out everything, but the man who owned the trailer, remember the man who yelled at us for trespassing and ordered us to get off his property?"

"Oh yeah, the creepy hick. I don't think I will ever forget that hillbilly."

"He was the one who killed James. He buried him in his back yard and then poured the concrete over his body to hide him. Thank goodness for your inquisitive mind. If it hadn't been for that, we never would have gotten a cadaver dog out there to search around."

"Dogs are amazing, they really are. Do you know where James was running to?"

"We don't know how much of the story to believe, but the man said he sent some people looking for James and found him in a small town near Palm Springs. James was the one who ditched his car near the road to throw us off. He had already found another girlfriend and was grooming her and her ... I'm not wanting to say this, but you deserve to know, her..."

I interrupted the detective and said, "Four-year-old daughter."

Good Lord, what is it with that age..

I can't say I'm sorry James is dead. The world is a safer place without him in it. Especially dark skinned and dark haired little four-year-old girls. *Makes me sick.*

I could tell Detective Joe was reaching his end of this conversation. He started pacing back and forth before me and then he wandered into the kitchen. This issue was making him nervous and it was at that moment I realized this was as hard on him as it was on me. Detective Joe really did have a big heart. Even the toughest men have a hard time dealing with the enormity of situations such as this one. I will ask him a few more questions and then let him have a break.

"Detective Joe please tell me about the truck drivers and the cameras."

"Those were a little tougher to figure out, but we think we finally have. The truck drivers were transporting the victims across state lines through California, Oregon, and Washington. The truck drivers were keeping these girls drugged and having their way with them for free. Sort of a freebie for transporting them for the group. Of course, they were also part of the trafficking ring."

"There is a large contingent we weren't aware of doing this, and now we are more aware and will be posting undercover agents at random truck stops across the country to try to get this under control. The surveillance cameras were just for the protection of the property of these homes. No security cameras, but still protecting what they considered their 'property,' which were the people, the victims, inside." They weren't people, they were commodities that they kept like pretty little drugged robots.

I hope these monsters burn in hell.

It's amazing all the weirdness that has passed through my little town. I wonder if it's because the freeway runs right through the middle of the city. Maybe that has something to do with it. I'm thinking back to the two serial killers who caused panic in our town, and now this. Our population is only around 100,000 people. I wouldn't consider it a huge metropolis by any means, but so much has happened here. I never expected this kind of thing could happen in my city. But why not my city? Where else should something like this happen? *How about nowhere.* Is there some kind of strange vortex or some kind of evil drawing evil back to this area? Perhaps there really is some powerful or mystical energy coming up out of the bowels of hell and passing through here. *I'm sure I will never know.* I may never know the answer, but something strange is going on around here. There's so much evil here. I'm sure the families of the victims will forever try to understand why, too. I felt like I stepped into a horror movie. I'm just glad I had a hand in bringing down the largest human trafficking and sex ring in North America.

Tonight, at least, my city is safe.

We obviously have a horrible criminal element here nobody wants to talk about. We have pimps looking for young kids to traffic. The youngest has been thought to be as young as eleven, but in James' case, even younger. These innocent children are trafficked in our country every single day. There's nothing done to address this issue. It's truly an epidemic. Before this happened to me, I had no idea it was anything nearly this big. This problem is so much bigger than people realize. I want to bring more awareness so everyone can come together and make a difference. We all need to work together to make a change for the better and save our children from these monsters.

When everything was said and done, the houses were empty, and boxes upon boxes of evidence and documents were removed. Because there was so much evil inside these homes, the detectives decided the best thing to do was destroy them. And that's exactly what they did. One by one, they are all gone, burned to the ground. I thought that was a very healing way to deal with all the evil that happened inside these homes.

I hope nothing ever gets built on the land where they once stood. I am a strong believer in good and bad energy, and the energy here will never be good. Even if you built another structure here, the land is still soaked with pure evil. The detectives have a long journey ahead of them. The last thing they said to me was, "We're going to make them pay for this. We're going to make them pay for all of this, and especially what they tried to do to you, Julie. This is a huge black mark against humanity."

I agree, that's exactly what this is, a mark against humanity. The lessons I learned through all of this were shocking. The methods these animals use to get their prey is sickening. Abducting and kidnapping an innocent four-year-old child to use in prostitution is horrific. Let me be clear, this is happening in our world today. *It happened to me.* I was trafficked by my own father at the age of four. Not only was I able to help bust the biggest sex trafficking ring in North America, I was also a victim of this horrible group. I had blocked it all out, and thankfully I got free and was able to live somewhat of a normal life.

Well, somewhat normal.

I still had an abusive mother and a lot of pain associated with that, however, nothing compared to what I would have experienced had my biological father not been killed. I owe everything to my real father for saving me. I mean the father who wanted to be my father and who adopted me at a young age. He never wanted me to know where I came from, and now I know why. I don't blame him, I probably would have done the same thing if I were in his shoes. I will never look at anyone in quite the same way, ever again.

Regardless of what kind of abuse I experienced by my mother, and the Catholic school I attended, I was still living a pretty sheltered life. I can't believe all the dignitaries that were involved with this, too. *Just to name a few.* Judges, priests *not surprised*, famous people, and even some police officers, were involved. To come to terms with the fact that it happened to me, how in the world did my mind block it all out? How can anyone look at a four-year-old child in a sexual way? I never want to know or understand. I guess it's true what the doctor said back in the emergency room. You would have to think like them to understand them, and you don't want to ever think like them.

I find it strange and extremely disturbing that this human trafficking group *cult* never forgot about me and came to where I work to try and get me back through James. It really gives me the creeps. He wasn't interested in me at all. He was just doing his job. As far as the child he was so excited about, that child, *my child*, would have been sold into this awful life. I believe I would have been as well. There definitely is a criminal element here in my little town that nobody wants to talk about.

But what about this horrible human trafficking ring? How did they manage to have so many docile victims? I was there on New Year's Day. None of these women tried to run or asked me for help. They certainly had many chances to. I have discovered that these cults, or rings, or whatever you want to call them … they rule by fear, intimidation and threats. They use drugs to keep the victims docile and in desperate need of them for their next drug fix. Daily physical abuse is prevalent. They also frequently move them all around the country to hide them away from prying eyes.

It's all about control. They are very much like a religious cult, although there's no religion at all, it's all about sex. They don't allow their victims to have any access to televisions, they're not allowed to watch any news stories, or spend any time on the internet. They are completely in the dark. This is a dangerous business to be on the other side of. They would've killed me in a heartbeat. I wonder how close I came to being killed. They killed their own, too. Just look where James is today. They have zero respect for human lives. I wouldn't be surprised if most of these victims miss their captors, like that Stockholm Syndrome Detective Joe told me about. They were extremely brainwashed and coerced by these monsters. I have heard there are certain groups out there, and the only way to join is to send a child molestation video. This stuff is beyond disgusting.

That brings me to this ... how does another human being reconcile doing this to another, especially a child? Not just the monsters that put innocent children to work in the sex trade, but what about the animals who purchase them? If there weren't any customers, maybe this wouldn't be going on. How does a person want to have sex with an innocent child? It completely disgusts me. How is a phrase like "human trafficking" even allowed to flourish in our society?

I have to have faith in humanity that we can end this once and for all. I have heard one very positive thing recently. I have heard of a group of truckers that have gotten together and formed a group of men fighting against human trafficking. I would like to personally thank them for their hard work. Keep fighting the fight until this is a thing of the past, just another black mark on humanity.

My story is not just a "moral to this story," it's a "listen to your intuition" as well. It's also a story that makes one think that just possibly it's true, everything happens for a reason. I never told anyone in my family I was helping the detectives. Especially not my family who didn't support me, anyway. A good Catholic family who sweeps everything under the carpet. Can't let all my mother's high society friends know about this. I couldn't risk anyone knowing. I couldn't trust anyone with this information. I never told any of my friends, either. Mary isn't my friend any longer. She will probably spend a long time in prison where she belongs, and I have no desire to visit her. Who fooled me the most? *Mary.*

When I look back on it all, I wonder, would I have ever changed any of it? I wished I hadn't gotten the abortion, and I'm still punishing myself for it. I may punish myself for the rest of my life. If I hadn't, though, would I have been put on this journey? Would I have been able to stumble on the hugeness of it all? I may never know the answer to that question. I will just have to rely on my own personal faith to get me through.

Many people, and not just creepy old men, were ordered to spend the rest of their lives in prison. And to think that just a nobody girl who worked as an admitting clerk in the largest trauma center on the

West Coast had a very important job in bringing it all down. One person can make a difference. One person can make a positive change in this world. I know firsthand that it's possible. If any of them ever get out of prison they won't be too happy with me for outing their sex ring. When or if that ever happens, I will probably have to go back into hiding.

But for now, I am free.

❧ 16 ❧

Today was Detective Joe's wedding day. I was so proud of him as he stood at the church altar. We shared a knowing glance and a smile while he waited for his bride to walk down the aisle. We have both been through so much, and now we belong to a very exclusive club. We could have never imagined the things we went through together. The magnitude of the great things we did will not go wasted on me. We will always be close friends and forever connected in a pretty amazing way.

It's really true, everything happens for a reason, the way it's supposed to. I was supposed to help put an end to the travesty of evilness that happened inside those homes. I am forever honored to have stood beside the brave men and women of this investigation. I learned some pretty horrific things about myself, but I wouldn't have changed a thing. If it had to hurt a little for me, it was worth it. We saved countless lives.

There is nothing I fear.

After the most beautiful wedding I have ever attended, I went home and straight to bed. It was late and I was tired. I had a dream I was holding a little boy. The baby I had aborted. I've had many dreams in the past, however, only a couple of my dreams so far have felt like actual visits. This last dream would be my third. The first vivid dream I had was from my grandma after a tragic event in my life. It was a few months after I had been raped by a stranger in college.

I was going through a very rough time, and was even feeling a bit suicidal. Not that I would have ever gone through with that, but let's just say it was a horrible time in my life. My grandma died when I was only six. I never attended her funeral because my parents thought I was too young. I had a very real dream about a visit from my grandma. I quit school about six months before. I was afraid the stranger who raped me would come back and kill me. I was afraid of this because he told me he would. I had wanted to be a doctor since the age of eleven, so this was a very tragic event in my early life. My attacker hadn't killed me, he just killed my dream of ever becoming a doctor instead.

This had to be the most incredible and vivid dream I have ever had. I was asleep in my bed in my new condo on a golf course. I woke up to the sound of someone knocking on my door. I got out of bed and then all of a sudden, I was hovering above my body watching myself walk down the stairs and toward the front door. As soon as I got to the front door, I was back inside my body again. *It was very strange.*

I opened the door and there stood my grandma. The very first thing she did was ... she reached her hand out to me, and asked me to take it. At first, I expected my hand to go right through hers, but it didn't. Her hand felt as solid to me as my own. Grandma held onto my hand the entire time she was with me. She led me outside and we walked down the driveway, through the parking lot. It was dark and deserted outside, just how one would imagine it would be in the middle of the night. She assured me that everything would be all right, and she was with me to help me get through this difficult time. She told me she loved me and had never left my side. It was the most reassuring dream I have ever had.

I never wanted it to end. After what felt like way too short of a time, Grandma told me our time was up. Grandma walked me back to my condo, gave me a kiss on the cheek, and started to walk away. I watched her walk away from my front door, and when she got to the edge of the parking lot next to the curb, she vanished. *She just disappeared.* I don't understand how it happened, but she walked across the street and then she just faded away. All of a sudden, I was back outside of my body again.

I watched myself walk up the stairs. When it was time to get back into bed, I was back inside my body. I woke up with the most peaceful feeling. I had to share the dream with my father the next day, because my grandma was also my father's mother. My adopted father, of course. He almost turned white when I described what Grandma Eva was wearing. *He also about fell off his chair.* I had perfectly described what she was buried in, right down to the crystal brooch she wore. Everything I described was what she wore when they buried her. In my heart I knew I had been visited by her, and my life got so much better after that dream.

Another dream that I consider to be real was the dream I had when my grandfather died. He had been sick for a long time and we knew his time was near. I was awakened from the dream I was having about him to be told he had just died. I already knew he had passed because I was with him. I was watching him from above as he skipped through a field of the biggest and most vibrant flowers I have ever seen. I remember yelling down at him, "Grandpa, what are you doing?"

"Isn't this the most beautiful place you have ever seen?"

"Yes, it is, but where are you going?"

He actually just giggled and kept floating along. He looked like he was skipping or frolicking through the most incredibly beautiful field of flowers. It's hard to explain what they looked like. First of all, they were huge, as tall as Grandpa, and the bloom was at least twice the size of his head. They were mostly white daisies. Giant white daisies. The grassy area just past the field of flowers was also vibrant green. Beyond the field of flowers was a grassy hill.

I couldn't see beyond the hill, but somehow, I instinctively knew I wasn't allowed to. Grandpa was on his way toward the hill when he was frolicking through the flowers. He was younger in appearance and his big stomach was completely flat. Grandpa had a liver disease that made his stomach appear bloated. Not anymore, he was young and healthy looking, too. I wished I could see what was past the bright hill of green, but I knew someday I would. I believe this was his entrance into Paradise. I'd never seen him this happy before, and to me he actually seemed euphoric. It warmed my heart, and I feel blessed to have been allowed to have had a glimpse. At least I was able to try to put some of his family at ease. The sad part is, I don't think most of them believed me. I know it was another visit.

And now, here I am having another one of my very real, very vivid dreams. This time, it's with my child that I had chosen to abort. He looked at me so sweetly and he said to me, "You absolutely did the right thing."

He used the same exact words the beautiful lady with bright red hair said to me at the clinic that day. "I'm on my way to be with a wonderful family. I was told I could come give you this message. I was able to move on and greatly rewarded in the process. Our souls will meet again when we go home someday. There are no hard feelings, there's only love and pride. No judgment, no shame. Dry your eyes and start to live again. We are the chosen ones. We choose our destiny. We chose this journey for reasons we will come to understand at another time. It wasn't the journey that mattered, it was the outcome. Because we chose our destiny, we were able to save many lives, and that is what really matters. We were chosen for this. There's nothing to fear anymore. There were others that were involved in making this decision with us. Many other souls had to sign off on the path we took. It will all be clear when we return home."

I hope this dream was real. It certainly felt as real as the dreams with my grandparents. To someone else this might sound crazy, and you'd most certainly think that I am, too. You'd have to have lived my life and seen the things I have in order to really fully understand. I'm an empathic medium, and perhaps that's why I was put here. It lends a new meaning to, "Everything happens for a reason." *Even abortion.*

Judge me if you must, I know I've done my fair share of it. All I can do is tell the story exactly as it happened ... *to me.* Please don't condemn me too much until you've walked in my shoes. I believe now, I had to lose my child to save my child.

Would I do it again?

I was able to save countless lives. But it was a very long and dark tunnel to go through. I'm proud I kept forging ahead. I felt guided to keep pushing on. Even as I write this story, I ask for guidance and the words to make a better impact on society. *The words to make a difference.* I don't consider myself a writer, but I do consider myself a storyteller.

Human trafficking is an epidemic of proportions beyond what anyone can imagine. It's still out there in every corner of the world. This is just the beginning. I'm proud we were able to help bring this huge ring down, but there's still so much more that needs to be done. There are so many other human trafficking rings out there in our world right now to conquer and destroy. All over the world this is still an epidemic that needs more light shined upon it. I hope that someday I can write another chapter about this. A new chapter letting everyone know it's over, and we have human trafficking finally in our rearview mirror.

Hopefully, never to return again.

I had one last visit with Detective Joe. He told me that I was soon going to be getting a reward, a medal of honor for helping them take down this disgusting ring. I told Joe I didn't need any medals or accolades, I was happy to help bring down something so evil.

"Julie, you don't have any idea how huge this is. First, you were born into this human trafficking cult, only to be sold to the highest bidder, and now you are hugely instrumental with bringing this whole thing down. Not just here, but worldwide. Don't you get what a big story this is?"

I guess he has a point. Maybe I would be insulting some people not to go to the award ceremony. My biggest concern was how to pay for the plane ticket, and my next biggest worry was getting on the plane. *I am terrified to fly.* However, how can I possibly be afraid of anything after all of this? I shouldn't fear anything anymore. Detective Joe thought it was so funny that I thought I would have to pay for the plane ticket. "No, dork, the grateful nation that wants to thank you will be buying your ticket."

Ok, ok I will go. Detective Joe was also honored, and we stood side by side. We actually never met the president but it was a moment in time I will never forget. I was so proud of us all. I used to joke that the only thing I could've written on my headstone was, "I told you I was sick." Now there's so much more to say. I made a positive impact on the world and I couldn't feel prouder. I just hope our efforts will inspire positive change in the world and put an end to this travesty of justice. It's time is long overdue.

In my opinion human trafficking absolutely is the new look of twenty-first century slavery. Let's not sugarcoat this issue. The victims desperately need us not to, and they need all of us to rally together to help them. The victims are as young as eleven, but unfortunately, even younger in some cases.

According to a book called *Renting Lacy*, the U.S. Department of Justice reports that 797,500 children (younger than eighteen) were reported missing in a one-year period of time. That's an average of 2,185 children per day. These kids are forced into a lifestyle they never chose. They are manipulated, abused, and tortured at the hands of the pimps who control them. Our country's children are sold on the streets, on the internet, and at truck stops across America every single day. These innocent children come from our neighborhoods, our schools, our churches, and sometimes, even our own homes.

The commercial sex industry, otherwise known today as forced prostitution, is worse than anyone, *including me,* could have ever imagined, and even harder to believe. Too many don't understand the severity and depth of this problem. I hope my book is the beginning of more understanding and opens up the conversation to put an end to this travesty once and for all. We are stronger and more capable than we realize.

We, together as a society, are too good to allow this behavior to continue. Our children depend on us to keep them safe. We mustn't let them down. This has to end, and it starts today with me. All people around the globe … join me to save the children of the world, our future lies in their hands. Let's stop letting them down. Rise up and end human trafficking. It's going to take us all working together to finally put an end to it. It's not someone else's job.

It's ours.

❧ ABOUT THE AUTHOR ❧

JULIE COONS lives in a small town in Oregon. THIS DOES NOT LEAVE THIS HOUSE was her debut memoir. Amy's bookshelf reviews awarded it the #1 position for top 10 books of 2018. Her second book WHY SHE LIED is based on a true story. Her books are written to lead a movement toward positive change. She tells the stories of her life with honesty and strength. If you wish to connect, ask a question, or invite Julie to speak to your group or organization, contact her at: connect@juliecoons.com. So much more coming in 2019! Julie also plans to make YouTube videos sharing more of her story. Subscribe to Julie's YouTube channel JULIE COONS and get to know her even better.

Website: juliecoons.com
YouTube: Julie Coons
Twitter: @JulieCoons1
Facebook: Julie Coons Author

❧ WHAT'S NEXT ❦

If you liked the book please tell your friends. Help me spread the word and put an end to human trafficking. I'd also be honored if you'd leave a review on Amazon.

***

I'd love to hear from you!
Please visit juliecoons.com and subscribe to my newsletter so you can become a preferred reader, get advanced notifications of book releases and enter giveaways to win prizes like a HD Kindle Fire Tablet.

Made in the USA
Middletown, DE
17 December 2020

28774319R00106